D0720936

*A Candlelight
Ecstasy Romance*®

"WHAT DO YOU THINK YOU'RE DOING?" MITCH DEMANDED.

"Very simple, Mr. Wranebow," Shannon said, dusting the chalk off her hands. "This is my side of the house, and that"—she pointed dramatically to the side he was standing on—"is yours."

"Do you think I'd live this way for the next month?" he asked incredulously.

"I do, and I'm warning you, Mitch, you step over that line just once without my permission and you'll run this resort by yourself. Our marriage is over, and let's keep it that way!"

"I wouldn't have you back on a gold platter, lady, so if you want to play this silly game, I'll abide by your rules!" he said haughtily. "Just remember, *you* made them, not me."

CANDLELIGHT ECSTASY ROMANCES ®

RAINBOW'S END

LORI COPELAND

A CANDLELIGHT ECSTASY ROMANCE®

Published by
Dell Publishing Co., Inc.
1 Dag Hammarskjold Plaza
New York, New York 10017

*To four very dear in-laws—Opal Copeland,
Maureen Copeland, Cathy Smart, and Marjorie Smart.
Needless to say, you are all very special to me.*

ISBN: 0-440-17239-X

Printed in the United States of America
First printing—December 1984

To Our Readers:

We have been delighted with your enthusiastic response to Candlelight Ecstasy Romances®, and we thank you for the interest you have shown in this exciting series.

In the upcoming months we will continue to present the distinctive, sensuous love stories you have come to expect only from Ecstasy. We look forward to bringing you many more books from your favorite authors and also the very finest work from new authors of contemporary romantic fiction.

As always, we are striving to present the unique, absorbing love stories that you enjoy most—books that are more than ordinary romance.

Your suggestions and comments are always welcome. Please write to us at the address below.

Sincerely,

The Editors
Candlelight Romances
1 Dag Hammarskjold Plaza
New York, New York 10017

CHAPTER ONE

"I'm sorry. Would you repeat that, please." Shannon gripped the telephone receiver tightly while her slender body started to tremble uncontrollably.

The deep voice on the other end of the phone spoke again as she slumped weakly down on the wicker barstool and closed her eyes painfully.

"How bad is it?" she asked in a soft frightened tone of voice.

"It could have been worse, Ms. Wranebow. They were both pinned in the wreckage for several hours before they were found. Your sister has several internal injuries, a cracked pelvis, numerous cuts and abrasions. . . ." The doctor paused and shuffled some papers noisily. "Your brother-in-law has four broken ribs, a punctured lung, and a compound fracture of the left leg, plus multiple lacerations all over his body. Right now they are both in intensive care, but we are hopeful they'll be able to be moved into a private room in another few days. Marla has been concerned about your being told of the accident and asked me to call you this morning."

"Thank you, Dr. Michaels. Please give her and Jerry my love, and tell her I'll leave sometime today. Do you happen to know who's looking after the resort?"

"I believe she has asked a neighbor to take over until

9

other arrangements can be made. I'm concerned that the responsibility of the resort is bearing heavily on their minds right now and should be turned over to someone else immediately. I think their recovery will be hampered if they aren't satisfied someone else has taken charge."

"Of course, I'll take care of all that as soon as I arrive," Shannon assured him shakily, her mind fighting to grasp the situation.

The sun was just beginning to rise over the horizon as she replaced the receiver back in its cradle and drew a long breath. Marla and Jerry had been in a serious car accident! Shannon pressed tense fingers against her temples trying to form some sort of organized plan in her mind. Marla had been more than a sister to her. Actually, she had assumed a Mother role in Shannon's life ever since their own mother had died fifteen years earlier. Being fifteen years old, she had felt lost and alone, turning to her twenty-year-old sister for comfort. She had never known her father, who had died before she was born. It seemed to her, as she stood in the pale morning sunlight, that she had spent most of her life losing someone she loved. For a brief moment a swift shaft of pain coursed through her heart as she mentally visualized a tall, ruggedly handsome man with black curly hair and eyes the blue of a morning glory just opening to the new day's light.

She rose slowly from the barstool and walked into her bedroom. Opening the closet door, she took out her suitcase and laid it on the bed. If she once let down her guard and let her mind dwell on Mitch, she would fall apart totally. Her hands paused in their packing as a disquieting thought assailed her. Good Lord! Would she have to see him again? She sank down on the bed, her mind

10

whirling rapidly. Of course, she would! Jerry was Mitch's brother. He might be on his way to Jerry and Marla's at this very moment! Shannon's fingers began to tremble as she removed her lingerie from the top drawer and laid it in the suitcase. What a complicated mess this could turn out to be. With a painful divorce behind her, she was most likely going to be thrown right back into her estranged husband's path, an occurrence she had avoided like the plague for the last few months. And even though they lived in the same town, it had been surprisingly easy.

Well, there was very little she could do about it at the moment. Maybe Mitch would be involved with his job right now and be unable to leave town, even for a few days. Picking up her bedside phone, she dialed the number of her office. It was still a few minutes before eight, but hopefully her secretary, Molly, would be in early this morning. When she and Mitch had separated last year, she had come back to her former job as the head buyer for ladies' fashions in a large department store here in St. Louis.

"Ms. Murphy's office," Molly answered in her slightly breathless voice. Shannon could picture her blond curls and wide innocent blue eyes as she spoke Shannon's maiden name.

"Hello, Molly, this is Shannon."

"Oh, Ms. Murphy, hi! Is there something wrong? I mean . . . this is the first morning I've *ever* beat you to work," she added lamely.

"Oh, Molly, I've just received some very upsetting news a few minutes ago. My sister and her husband were in an automobile wreck yesterday, and I'm going to have to go down there. Cancel all my appointments for this week, and don't reschedule any of them until I call you."

Shannon bit her lower lip pensively. "I have no idea how long I'll be gone." Luckily she had several weeks vacation she hadn't taken and a very understanding boss.

"I'm so sorry, Ms. Murphy," Molly sympathized. "Don't you worry about a thing on this end. I'll call Jackie and tell her. Between the two of us we'll keep things running smoothly until you return."

"Thanks, Molly. I'll give Jackie a quick call myself before I leave, but it would be wise for you two to talk before she comes in." Jackie Arnold was Shannon's left hand at the office. Between her and Molly, Shannon felt secure in leaving for a few days. Even though Molly presented the stereotyped picture of a dumb blonde, she was far from that category. Shannon would match her with any secretary in the state for efficiency!

"I'll check with you after I stop at the hospital," Shannon said absently as she debated over whether to drive or fly. It would be a good five-hour drive from here to the small resort town where Jerry and Marla had bought their tourist resort last year. She knew she could charter a small plane that would land at the School of the Ozarks some fifteen miles away, but she would be left without any means of transportation to get her around. No, it would probably be better to make the drive.

"I'll be waiting for your call. . . . And Ms. Murphy . . . I hope everything turns out all right. . . ." Molly faltered.

"It will. . . ." Shannon swallowed hard, blinking back rising tears in her luminous brown eyes. She would not allow herself to think of the alternative. Replacing the phone in its cradle gently, she allowed herself the luxury of letting the tears slip down her cheeks for one brief moment. Funny, I wouldn't think there were any tears left to fall, she thought fleetingly. She had cried enough tears the last year to last her for a lifetime.

Wiping the wetness from her cheeks swiftly, she made a hurried call to Jackie, then loaded her suitcases in the back of her sporty black Porsche. Within thirty minutes of the doctor's call, Shannon was on the way.

Ten hours, one flat tire, and a busted water hose later, she was tiredly watching for the turnoff leading to Wranebow's Inn.

At the time her sister moved here, Shannon had thought that Marla and Jerry had totally lost their minds when they quit their jobs—Jerry, a rising executive in the steel industry and Marla, a successful fashion model—and sunk their life savings in a run-down resort in the foothills of the Ozark Mountains.

In the growing twilight of the humid July evening, Shannon could easily see the beauty of the scenic Ozarks. Thick green foliage covered the hillsides, and the sound of jarflies and katydids shattered the silence as Shannon turned off the main highway onto Road DD. Driving along in the gathering dusk, she could see the outline of the lake and a long gleaming bridge spanning the water. The ominous, black storm clouds that had followed her for the last fifty miles hovered close to the water now, bright streaks of lightning flashing occasionally from their churning depths. These summer storms could be very violent, and Shannon hoped she would be safely tucked away at the resort before this particular storm finally broke.

The Porsche sped along in the darkening gloom, the first few sprinkles of rain splashing sparsely on the windshield. The tempo of the rain began to pick up, and suddenly the heavens opened wide, sending a virtual downpour gushing forth.

Shannon reached to turn on the windshield wipers and groaned in despair when she saw the worn out blade she had been meaning to replace come to life and feebly try to wipe off the onslaught of water sloshing down on the dust-splattered glass. She braked suddenly, her field of vision totally obscured now. The wiper was making a muddy smear across the path it followed. Sliding up on the front of her seat, she tried to peer through the small slit at the bottom of the windshield, meeting with little success.

The unfamiliar road and the strain of the approaching storm had drawn her nerves into a tight knot, her eyes growing strained from their tense scrutiny of the winding road before her.

Glancing up nervously in her rearview mirror, she saw the lights of a fast-approaching car. She belatedly flipped on her own lights, growing more desperate by the minute. The time had come when she was either going to have to roll down her window and stick her head out to see, or pull over and park until the rain let up. She knew it couldn't be more than a mile to her destination according to Marla's directions in a previous letter. If she could just make it a little farther, she would be home free! With a sigh of desperation, she rolled down her window and stuck her head out. The pelting rain hit her in the face and drenched her light sun-kissed brown hair.

The car behind her was approaching swiftly as the driver gave a loud impatient blare of his horn and swung out around her in an agitated manner. As his wheels spun past her car, she gasped in astonishment when a gigantic puddle of muddy water was splashed rudely in her face

14

by the streaking car. Sputtering wildly for air, she fought to hold the small car on the road. Good grief! She moaned irritably, bringing her car nearly to a halt in the road. Was that guy nuts! The taillights of the elegant car braked while signaling to make a left turn off the road.

Muddy, oily water dripped down Shannon's face making her nearly gag from the vile mixture of dirt, asphalt, and road tar. In disgust she started the Porsche moving again slowly, her eyes searching out the sign on the left side of the road that read, Wranebow's Inn Five Hundred Yards.

Gunning the car defiantly, and in spite of the fact that she could barely see, Shannon flew down the road in a cloud of smoke. That road hog needed a piece of someone's mind, and she was just the person to give it!

As she skidded beside the now-still black Mercedes parked in front of the inn, she braked, sending a spray of gravel over the docile vehicle. Reaching for the door handle, she tumbled out heatedly, making her way over to the other car, revenge blazing in her eyes. She reached down and jerked open its door, her eyes widening in astonishment as she came face-to-face with her ex-husband, Mitchell Wranebow.

"You idiot," she sizzled. "Do you know what you just did?"

A guarded look of lazy amusement spread over Mitch's face as he replied tauntingly, "Why, if it isn't my cute little blushing bride. Have I done something to upset you *again*, dear?"

"You nearly drowned me, you big klutz!" she railed, coming precariously close to tears now. "Just look at me!" She stepped back giving him a better view of her wet mud-covered blouse and soggy jeans, her eyes staring daggers at him. The fact that he was sitting in a nice dry car while she was standing in the rain did nothing to assuage her anger.

He got out of his car slowly, towering ominously over her five-foot-one frame. His eyes ran suggestively up and down her rain-soaked body, lingering longer than necessary on her breasts that were straining enticingly through her wet blouse.

"Why, I was just thinking how lovely you looked tonight," he stated calmly. His gaze refused to leave her breasts, and she felt herself flush at his blatant scrutiny. In defiance, she wrapped her arms in front of her. A large aching knot grew in her stomach as they stood in the dark stormy night looking into each other's familiar faces. Her eyes locked with his beautiful blue ones, and she couldn't help but recall the hundreds of times they had gazed back at her with unquenchable desire.

"How are you, Shannon?" His voice was soft and deep as he spoke her name, sending an avalanche of painful memories crowding through her mind.

The fight drained out of Shannon, her knees turning to pure jelly as the reality of Mitch standing before her hit home. She hadn't seen him in a very long time, and his totally masculine appearance unnerved her. From the moment she had met Jerry Wranebow's younger brother, she had instantly and deeply fallen in love with him. They were drawn together as a moth is to a flame and married after a brief whirlwind courtship. For the first two months of their marriage, they had been head over heels in love with each other. Shannon had walked around with her head in the clouds, scarcely able to believe that so much happiness could be hers. If only that dream could have lasted . . . if only he had listened to reason and not insisted on continuing a profession that would risk his life day after day. . . .

Standing here now, their eyes hungrily drinking in the sight of each other, she wondered once more if the divorce had been worth it. Wouldn't it have been less painful to have lost him to an accident, but still have the beautiful memories of him, than to live day after lonely day without him, knowing that somewhere he was existing in a world without her? She still didn't have the answer to that question.

Shannon fought to clear her head and break the emotional gaze that seemed to have them both momentarily paralyzed. She drew a long breath. How was she? She was dying inside; but he would never know it.

"What are you doing here, Mitch?" she blurted mindlessly.

A look of surprise flickered briefly across his face before his eyes turned to icy disdain, his features turning hard and unrelenting. "I'm here for the same reason you are," he said flatly.

Shannon turned from him, walked to the trunk of her car, and inserted the key. "Then, I'm sure you'll want to be on your way to the hospital *and* to rent a hotel room. It's getting late." Very late, she thought resentfully. If she had the good sense God gave a goose, she would turn around and go back home . . . immediately!

Stepping up on the small porch of the tiny cottage, Shannon slammed her bag down, pushing her dripping wet hair back from her face. She knelt down, running her hand under the rubber welcome mat lying in front of the screen door. Marla had once told her there was an extra key kept there, and since Shannon would not be going to the hospital until later this evening, she had to get into the house.

"That's strange," Shannon mumbled irritably, running her hand back and forth under the mat. "She said they always kept one here!" Shannon was crawling back and forth now on her knees, becoming increasingly agitated. She was cold, tired, her wet clothes molding to her body like a second skin. Large goose bumps were popping out all over her now, making her shiver inwardly, and adding one more miserable thing to her list of growing discomforts.

Mitch stepped up calmly on the porch, watching her growing frustration with cool tranquility. After several moments of watching her search in vain, he stepped over her unconcernedly, removing a key from the pocket of his perfectly tailored, charcoal-colored slacks, inserted the key into the locked door, opened it, and flipped on the light switch, illuminating the cottage with a soft glow of yellow light. Shannon's mouth dropped open as he stepped into the room, closing the door firmly behind him.

Springing to her feet in disgust, Shannon threw open the door with a less than ladylike entrance. "How in the devil did you get a key?" she asked sarcastically, dirty water running in puddles around her feet.

Mitch was sitting serenely on the couch, stretching his long frame out more comfortably before him. He glanced up with a smug look skipping across his handsome features. "I stopped by the hospital on the way over here," he said with an infuriating grin. "By the way, Marla said to tell you she was sorry, but there's no longer an extra key under the mat. Jerry had to use it in an emergency one day and never put it back."

Shannon brought her hands up to her slender hips in an agitated stance. "Why couldn't you have told me that instead of letting me crawl around on that mat like a dog!" she said coldly.

Mitch turned accusing aloof blue eyes on her. "You wouldn't have believed me. If you recall, Mrs. Wranebow," he said pointedly, "you haven't believed a word I've said for the last year."

With a tired sigh, Shannon let her hands fall from her hips slowly, her gaze avoiding him purposely. "You haven't *told* me the truth in a year," she said wearily.

"That's an old record, Shannon, and personally, I'm tired of hearing it." Mitch rose to his feet swiftly and walked over to the large picture window that faced the lake to stare moodily out into the rainy night.

The air in the room grew tense as Shannon willed herself to ignore his goading comments. She turned on her heel and marched back out on the porch to retrieve her wet luggage. He was not going to draw her into another shouting match! After every heart-searing painful encounter they had been through since their separation, she had come away with more resentment and anger than before. She was tired of the hurt and tears and wanted nothing more than to forget the man who stood before her. Days of peace and tranquility were what she longed for, days without the remembrance of what could have been.

With a determined mental shake of her head, she picked up her suitcase and stepped back into the dimly lit family room/kitchen. A tender smile emerged from her lips as she stood for a moment, her eyes roaming over the room before her. So this was Marla and Jerry's home. Such a beautiful secure marriage they had together—

19

each one totally dedicated to the other one. This was the first time Shannon had been to their new home. Marla had begged her to come and visit them, but Shannon had buried herself in her work, discreetly refusing her sister's invitations. The last thing in the world she wanted was to be reminded of Mitch, and Jerry would have been a very painful reminder of him. Both brothers had the same handsome characteristics—dark curly hair, rugged tanned features—with the exception of their eyes. Mitch had unusual clear sky-blue ones, while Jerry had dark, soft chocolate-brown eyes.

Shannon could feel Marla's presence in this comfortable, attractive room. She could envision long winter nights when Jerry and Marla had undoubtedly shared passionate moments in front of the massive rock fireplace that stretched widely across one whole wall. Shelves of books lined the floor-length bookcases flanked on either side of it. Casual, earth-tone-colored sofa and chairs were positioned around the center of the room, and heavy, dark oak tables gleamed in the mellow lamplight. A couple could sit on the sofa and stare at the flickering flames, then feast their eyes on the glistening water of the lake beyond the sweeping expanse of glass draped tastefully in panels of beige, brown, and rust. It was a room decorated with love, and in Marla's marriage there was an overabundance of that. Why couldn't it have been like that for her and Mitch, she pondered sadly as her eyes once again focused on the tall, black-headed man standing at the window brooding silently. It wasn't for the lack of love on her part, because she had loved him more than any one person deserved to be loved. If only she could have learned to live with the fact that he wanted to continue in his family's business when his father was killed in a job-related accident, they would still be together. She could never have been happy living that way, but at least she would be able to reach out and touch him during the long lonely nights.

Mitch turned from his stance at the window, a shadow of bleakness visible on his face. Seeing Shannon standing in the middle of the room drew him back to the present, a cold mask of indifference covering his sorrowful look.

"You said you stopped by the hospital," Shannon began. "How . . . Has there been any change?"

He reached up absently to run his fingers tiredly through his thick hair. Shannon noticed there were new lines in his face, tense worried lines that hadn't been there the last time she saw him. He would soon be thirty-eight years old, and if anything, he was more attractive than ever. It just wasn't fair, she thought resentfully. At the moment she was painfully aware she looked every ounce her thirty years.

"No—no change. I spoke with the doctor, and he said they were progressing slowly, and that the way he sees it they should be laid up for at least a month. Jerry's so damn worried about this resort, he won't listen to the doctor's orders and forget business!"

"I know, but everything they have is wrapped up in this venture. I've got to try to find someone to run it for them for a while," she murmured thoughtfully.

"Well, I hope you come up with someone who'll work free. Jerry said they didn't have the cash to pay a salary to anyone," Mitch told her grimly.

"Their financial situation is *that* precarious?" Shannon was stunned at the news. Marla had told her the first few years would be rocky, but she never dreamed they would have to cut it that close.

21

"Apparently . . . anyway, I told them not to worry. I'd figure out something. The last thing they need is the worry that their business might fail. It looks like we'll have to run the damn thing ourselves!" he speculated grimly.

"Don't be ridiculous!" she snapped crossly. "You have your own business obligations, and I have mine."

"Have you ever heard of the word *sacrifice*, Shannon! Hell! My brother's lying up there in the hospital close to death, and you think I'm going to turn around and walk out on him when he needs me? *You* are the only one in this family who takes a walk when the going gets tough!" he sneered.

"That's not fair, Mitch!" Shannon felt her stomach tighten into a knot at the reference to their own problems. "This is an entirely different situation. I wouldn't walk out on Marla. I love her!" she defended hotly.

"Really! Well, you claimed you loved me, too, but that didn't stop you from walking out on me, lady!" he exploded.

"We were not discussing *our* relationship, Mitch. And, besides, I had every reason to walk out on you—and you know it!" Shannon dug her nails into her palms painfully, wondering why he was going into all of this right now.

"Every reason!" Mitch's voice dipped to a low angry timbre. "I can't ever remember giving you *anything* but my love, Shannon. All of it! But you thought so little of our marriage you let this business of me staying in Dad's firm until this *one* contract is completed—"

"Or until you killed yourself!" Shannon interrupted angrily.

"That's ridiculous and you know it!" he returned tightly. "You forget I've been raised in the steel business.

Just because I promised to get out of it when we got married doesn't mean I'm some greenhorn who doesn't know his rear end from a hole in the ground!"

"You promised the day we were married you'd get out of that risky job, but you didn't! You used the excuse of your father's illness—"

"He was ill! Are you saying a heart attack isn't an illness?" he asked incredulously.

"No! I know Clinton was sick, but that didn't stop *me* from dying a little every day you went to work, Mitch! Then, your father wasn't back to work two weeks before . . ."

"Before he fell," Mitch said in a tormented groan.

"Before he . . . fell," Shannon agreed painfully. "I couldn't live through another year and a half always wondering when the phone rang if it would be you next. . . ."

Shannon turned from him and walked over to a kitchen chair, sinking down tiredly. Her hands felt like blocks of ice as her mind forced her back to the day that she had stood with Mitch and stared up at what seemed to her miles of steel disappearing into the leaden sky. She could almost feel the sting of the cold wind biting through her heavy jacket as Mitch had drawn her tenderly into his arms for warmth.

"I *have* to finish the job for him, sweetheart," he had whispered against her ear painfully. "This was his dream. It's up to me to see it through." Shannon remembered leaning back against his solid chest, her hand tightening around his. They had buried Clinton Wranebow that morning, and she knew the agony Mitch felt. But to think of her love, her very life, working every day on a building project that could very well take *his* life . . .

just as it took his father's . . . a rippling shudder ran through her small frame. No! He couldn't do this to her!

"No, Mitch, no!" she had begged softly, her hands squeezing his in anxiety. "I know how you must be feeling now, but you can't do this to me—to us! You promised you'd take a desk job at the office!"

"Shannon, sweetheart, I know you're afraid, but *nothing* will happen to me," he soothed, kissing her ear gently. "I know how my job upsets you, but I'm the only one who can carry on Dad's dream right now, and . . . damn it, Shannon, this is something I *have* to do. Please don't fight me on this," he pleaded fervently as he buried his face in the fragrance of her neck. "As soon as the building's completed, I'll take that nice, safe desk job."

A cold knot of fear had risen in Shannon's stomach as she stood gazing up at the steel monster that had been predicted to take at least seven men's lives before completion. It had already claimed its first victim, and it was barely in the first stages of construction. How long before it would come for its second conquest? Somehow, someway, she would have to stop him from throwing his life away! But, as the weeks passed, she couldn't stop him. Her fear grew and festered until one day it was no longer tolerable. Shannon Wranebow took the bull by the horns and issued an angry ultimatum. Either Mitch step out of the picture and let someone else run the job, or she would *not* be around to bury him. It had not taken but a matter of days for Shannon to realize Mitchell Wranebow did *not* accept ultimatums. The divorce became final months later without contest.

"Mitch, please . . ." she said, trying to push the painful memories into the back of her mind. "I don't want to go over this again. We were talking about Marla and Jerry's problems. It doesn't matter any longer who was right or who was wrong." Shannon fought against the rising tears, taking an angry swipe at them as they slipped down her cheeks.

"You're right," he agreed passively, "I'm sorry. I didn't mean to drag up the past. Our marriage is over . . . and I couldn't be happier."

Shannon's heart thudded painfully at his curt words. She was glad the marriage was over, too, but did he have to be so . . . glib about it? "Not any happier than I am," she couldn't resist answering.

"By the way, Shannon," Mitch said as he strolled casually over to where she sat and dropped down in the chair next to her, "have you found a nice *safe* man yet? One that you will have *no* doubt will always walk in the door every night?"

Shannon glared at him silently.

"Now, don't get that mean look on your face," he said in an amiable voice, "I was just wondering about you. It seems that our paths haven't crossed . . . not once . . . in the last four months." He looked at her pointedly.

"You noticed? I'm flattered. No, I haven't found a man, yet," she said, smiling, "but I'm still looking." If he wanted to pick a fight, he would have to look elsewhere.

"Well, maybe while I'm here, I can help you work on it. Two heads are always better than one." He smiled back.

"Why don't you just let me worry about my men?" she said curtly.

"That's a good idea. You were always good at worrying," he agreed readily.

"Drop dead, Mitch," she said childishly, getting up and walking over to her suitcase.

Mitch rose to his feet and looked at her in mock consternation. "Drop dead! Why I thought that was what this whole divorce was about, trying to keep me from 'dropping dead.' Now you're telling me you want me to?"

"I'm not telling you anything except to move out of my way. I'm tired and I want to rest before I go to the hospital." Shannon picked up her suitcase and stared up angrily at her cocky adversary.

His features softened as he gazed back into her pretty, flushed features. "Would you like to 'rest' together?" he suggested with a devilish grin. "The bedroom is right in there," he said, pointing to the closest open door.

Shannon shoved past him rudely and walked toward the bedroom, deliberately ignoring his sexual innuendo.

Mitch shrugged his broad shoulders and dropped back down in his chair. "I didn't figure you would." He leaned his head back and closed his eyes as he heard the bedroom door slam.

It was barely a few minutes later before the bedroom door swung back open and Shannon approached his chair again.

He opened one eye and arched his brow. "You change your mind?"

"*I'm* not that hard up for a man, Mitch. We need to discuss how we're going to do this!" Her voice was level and very stern.

"Anyway you want to 'do it.'" He smirked. "It so happens *I* am hard up for a woman at the moment!"

"That is not what I meant, and you know it!"

If she hadn't known it before now, she no longer had any doubts. This was going to be one heck of a long night!

26

CHAPTER TWO

Their eyes locked boldly with each other's in defiance for a moment before Mitch gave a cocky mock salute to her and backed off. "I have to tell you, Shannon, my next wife is going to have *none* of your hotheaded worrisome characteristics," he said bluntly.

"And my next husband is going to be an orderly in a hospital, as ugly and undesirable as a mud fence and willing to listen to reason. We should both be happy," she replied calmly.

"All right." He let out a short breath, then dismissed her completely. "Now, back to what we were originally discussing. I don't know about you, but I won't have any problems getting away for a few weeks. My crew should be able to carry the load for that long. What's your situation?"

"My situation on what?" she asked suspiciously, sitting down.

"On getting away for a while. *I'm* willing to take my brother's share of the work around here. Are *you* willing to take your sister's place?" he challenged.

"You're kidding!" she said disbelievingly.

"Do you have a better idea?" he asked.

"Well . . . no . . . but I sure hadn't thought about

the two of *us* trying to run this place," she sputtered helplessly.

"Then, I suggest you start thinking in that vein. Obviously, we're the only *free* candidates at the moment."

"Are you suggesting that we *live* here in this house . . . together . . . and try to run this resort? Why that's the most preposterous suggestion you've conjured up yet! In the first place, I wouldn't begin to know how to manage a tourist resort; secondly, I wouldn't stay under the same roof with you for thirty minutes; let alone thirty days and thirdly, you don't know any more than I do about this place! We would have everything in chaos within a week!" Shannon couldn't believe he would even suggest such an undertaking. They were both strictly "city dudes"!

"Hell, I could run this place with one hand tied behind my back," Mitch scoffed arrogantly. "How much do you have to know to be able to rent out a few rooms and keep the grass mowed?"

"I don't know, Mitch. . . ." Shannon wasn't sure how much actual work would be involved, but she was sure there was more than met the eye. Marla had complained of near exhaustion in her recent letters. "Besides, what about the living arrangements?" she argued.

He put his hand on his lean hip and looked at her sarcastically. "Are you worried that I'll try to make a pass at you? Well, don't be. You've lost *all* of your appeal to me. I was only heckling you a few minutes ago."

Shannon glared at him snidely. "Do you *really* expect me to believe that! I happen to know what a . . . a hot pants you are! You're still a man, aren't you?" she scoffed.

28

"Beats me. You want to check it out?" He grinned suggestively.

Shannon's eyes dropped from his gaze. She hated it when he came on all virile and sexy like that! When they were married and he began to tease her with that tone of voice, it wasn't long before he hauled her off to the bedroom! Well, she might be forced into staying here with him until Marla and Jerry recovered, but she would not submit herself to his oversexed manly ego!

"I wouldn't know either"—she smiled sweetly—"nor do I care to find out."

Mitch cast a knowing smirk at her. "You're whistling a different tune than you used to, lady. I seem to remember dragging into my office, completely worn out morning after morning from your . . . uh . . . 'indifference,' " he taunted. "Now, are you going to help or not?"

Her countenance grew stormy as she faced him impatiently. "All right! If I have to, I'll accept my share of responsibility; but *just* to insure that you'll have the strength to carry out your 'sacrificial role as a devoted brother,' we'll just make sure I don't take advantage of your extreme"—she looked at him snidely—"susceptibility in the bedroom." Snatching up a piece of chalk from the board next to the kitchen wall phone, she measured the room off with her blazing brown eyes. With a quick efficient movement, she proceeded to draw a white line down the middle of the room with the chalk.

Mitch stood with his arms crossed, watching her with a tight, appraising glare. "What in the hell do you think you're doing?" he asked skeptically.

"Very simple, Mr. Wranebow," she said, dusting the chalk off her hands on her muddy jeans. "This is my side of the house, and that," she pointed dramatically to the

29

side he was standing on, "is yours. As long as we stay here together, do not—I repeat—do not step over that line unless you're asked," she warned grimly. "And you won't be asked!" she added.

Mitch's eyes followed the straight white line down the center of the room disgustedly. "That's about the most childish thing I've ever seen you do. Do you honestly think I'd live this way for the next month? You can't be serious!"

"I drew the line, didn't I?" she returned staunchly.

"You do realize that in order for me to get to the kitchen I'd have to step over that damn line, don't you?"

"We all have our problems, Mitch," she returned hostilely.

He uncrossed his arms and glanced around the room appraisingly. "Of course, *you* are going to have to cross the line to get to the bathroom!" he noted gleefully.

Shannon's face fell as she glimpsed the hall to the bathroom on *his* side of the room. "Okay," she relented easily, "I'll trade you one hour in my kitchen a day in exchange for an hour in your bathroom every day. How's that?"

"You're not going to cook for me?"

"You don't miss a thing, do you?" she said brightly.

Mitch shrugged his broad shoulders indifferently. "That's no big sacrifice. You're a lousy cook, if I remember correctly."

"Your memory's excellent," she praised lavishly. "I *am* a horrible cook. I'm also hotheaded, overdemanding in bed, and a bitchy, worrisome wife! Have I left out anything?"

"You've got a smart mouth!" he muttered tightly.

"Sorry . . . and I've got a smart mouth," she added

30

obediently. "Now, if you have no objections, I'm going to take a hot bath and go to bed. I've decided to go to the hospital early tomorrow morning." Mitch moved aside as she started toward the hall. "You sleep in the bedroom closest to your side of the line," she ordered curtly.

"You're not afraid to stay under the same roof with me?" he heckled. "After all, I'm such a 'hot pants' . . . according to you."

"I'm not worried," she said lightly. "I'm more than able to defend myself."

"I'd be happy to stop by WalMart's and pick up a chastity belt for you tomorrow," he persisted in a tormenting tone. "You'd probably rest easier if you knew I wouldn't come in and attack you in the middle of the night!"

She paused and turned back to face him. "You just be sure *you* stay on your side of the line. That's all I'll worry about. And by the way, Mitch, since we'll be forced to live under the same roof for the next few weeks, I insist on having my privacy. Instead of 'Oh, Shannon' or 'Hey, you,' you are to knock on my door if you want to speak with me."

Mitch gave a snort of disbelief. "What door?" he asked sarcastically.

Shannon whirled back around and marched back to the kitchen. She exaggeratedly drew an imaginary doorway in the air with her fingertip, then turned back around and marched past him once again. *"That door,"* she tossed over her shoulder as she strolled down the hall to the bathroom.

"Now I know you're nuts!" Mitch yelled at her retreating back, his eyes still surveying the boundary line. "You really don't expect me to take this seriously, do you?"

"I'm warning you, Mitch," she said, still striding toward her destination. "You step over that line just *once* without my permission, and you'll find yourself running this resort all by yourself. I'll do anything to help Marla and Jerry *except* 'play house' with you! Our marriage is over . . . let's keep it that way!"

"I wouldn't have you back on a gold platter, lady, so if you want to play this silly damn game, I'll abide by your rules!" he said haughtily. "Just remember, though, *you* made them, not me."

"I'll remember," she said, slamming the bathroom door loudly. That was the problem, she muttered to herself as she angrily opened her suitcase; she couldn't forget!

Bright sunshine flooding her bedroom awoke Shannon early the next morning. She was nearly as tired as when she had gone to bed. The unfamiliar bed had made her toss and turn the whole night. She knew Mitch had spent a miserable night, also, since she had heard him get up several times to prowl on his side of the house restlessly. Closing her eyes for a moment, she savored the delicious feeling of just being in the house with him once again.

With an absent sigh she slipped out of bed, silently picking up a pair of red shorts and a cool top, and crept softly into the bathroom, trying to be as quiet as possible. The door to Mitch's room was closed, and she assumed he was still sleeping.

Washing her face with a large fluffy washcloth, she quickly applied a light coat of makeup, then brushed her unruly curls hurriedly, groaning as she saw all the rebellious ends sticking up as a result of her night of fighting with the unfamiliar pillow. She picked up her toothbrush and squirted a gob of blue gel onto it before brushing vigorously. Staring back at her reflection in the mirror, she decided that she definitely was not looking her best this morning.

She tiptoed out into the kitchen, put on a pot of coffee, then opened the kitchen door and let herself out into the clean rain-washed air. Breathing in deeply the fresh smell of the early summer morning, she stood spellbound as her eyes focused on the breathtaking view from the red-wood deck of the house. The lake lay shimmering like a rare jewel in the early morning light, the water peacefully lapping at the quiet shores. A lone sailboat, its white sails ruffling in the slight breeze, sat bobbing in the still water. The birds chattered noisily in the trees as the woodpeckers busily made their rat-a-tat-tat on the wooden telephone poles. Squirrels were happily making their way from tree to tree, dropping their acorns in a boisterous fashion on top of the mobile homes sitting quietly in the trailer park next to Jerry and Marla's resort, their occupants still soundly sleeping.

Shannon drew in another deep breath, closing her eyes for a moment. She could see why Marla had fallen so in love with the Ozarks. Never had Shannon experienced such a calm and tranquil feeling as she did now, standing in this quiet paradise, the lush green hills and valleys surrounding her.

She opened her eyes slowly, seeing the rows of cottages to her left. Their fresh coat of avocado paint was trimmed in black, and they looked clean and well cared for. Jerry and Marla had worked long, backbreaking hours painting and restoring this resort. When they had first bought it, it was in a state of ruin. They had hammered, nailed, painted, poured concrete, fixed leaky roofs, planted flower gardens, sown endless sacks of grass seed. . . . Everything Marla had written to her about was in plain view before her. Shannon could see the large vegetable garden Marla so lovingly cared for over to her right; the tomatoes hanging fat and plump on the vines. A well-fed contented rabbit sat munching on one of the tender plants, enjoying the fruits of Marla's hard labor.

There was a large swimming pool which lay in the center of the cottages, its blue water glistening in the early morning sun. Several picnic tables, with a large outdoor grill, sat under a covered pavilion. Badminton nets and a shuffleboard court surrounded the picnic area, offering their guests a variety of activity in the long summer evenings.

Nestled between two majestic oaks hung a large wooden porch swing facing the lake. Marla had told Shannon that she and Jerry had spent endless hours sitting out there in the evenings, listening to the jarflies and katydids, dreaming and planning their future together.

Shannon exhaled a wistful sigh thinking of Jerry and Marla's blissfully happy marriage, wishing with all her heart that she could have been as fortunate in her own marriage.

Her eyes became misty as she thought of the long, painful recuperation period that faced Jerry and Marla. Things could be a whole lot worse, she scolded herself as she reached over to pick one of the profusely blooming roses trailing up the side of the porch. Holding the flower to her nose, she breathed in its fragrant perfume, revelling in its glorious scent. One of them could have lost the other, and that would have been unthinkable.

Her attention was diverted from the lovely morning as she heard Mitch stirring around in the house. Casting one last appreciative glance at her surroundings, she stepped back into the house quietly. Her breath caught momentarily as her eyes fastened on Mitch just coming out of his bedroom wearing only a pair of gray slacks he had worn the night before. His broad chest was bare, exposing the thick black hair that tapered off slightly at his slim waist. His powerful arms and back showed tight corded muscles, flexing slightly with each movement as he walked across the room. His black curly hair was tousled appealingly from sleep, his eyes a lazy sensual blue as he grunted a barely civil "Knock-knock, good morning" to her as he saw her standing framed in the early morning light.

"Good morning," she whispered, her throat growing tight and restricted as she stood hungrily drinking in the sight of his half-naked physique. Erotic memories flooded her mind cruelly as she recalled all the times she had lain in those powerful arms, her face buried passionately in that heavy dark hair on his chest. A surge of longing rushed through her before she could manage to tear her eyes from Mitch reluctantly. These kinds of thoughts would get her nowhere!

"Are you through in the bathroom?" he asked politely, his eyes lingering on her slender bare legs for a fraction of a minute before meeting her disturbed gaze.

"Yes, thank you," she murmured. She moved on into the kitchen and went to the cabinet for a coffee cup. Her hands were unsteady as she poured a cup of the fresh coffee and sat down weakly at the table.

"Then, if you'll excuse me, I'll take my shower." His tall, husky form disappeared back into the hall, and Shannon momentarily heard the bathroom door close.

Burying her face in her hands, she fought the overwhelming feeling to scream out all of her pent-up frustrations over him. This arrangement would never work out. Just seeing him a few minutes ago had unnerved her to the point of hysteria. He had always been able to turn her to putty in his hands by merely one sexy look from those heavenly blue eyes. And he knew it! That's what scared her about this whole impossible situation. If he did try to make love to her, would she have the stamina to refuse him? At the moment the answer was a miserable no! She mentally damned her foolish, feminine weakness for him. With other men Shannon was able to take them or leave them, but with Mitch she was a spineless, trembling fool. And she had thought she was finally getting over him. What a big, cruel joke!

The door to the bathroom swung open, and a devastatingly handsome Mitch came down the hall and paused on his side of the room. His tantalizing after-shave filled the kitchen, adding one more hurtful memory to Shannon's ever-growing list. Glancing at the fresh perked pot of coffee, he turned earnestly pleading eyes on her. "Knock-knock."

Feeling a little ashamed of the childish way she had been acting, she extended an olive branch. "Help yourself to the coffee. The cups are in the right-hand side of the cabinet."

He flashed her an infectious grin, replying in his most exaggerated John Wayne cowboy drawl, "Thanks, ma'am. Do ya mind if I set at yur table to eat my vittles this mornin'? I feel like my horse has been aridin' *me* all night!"

Shannon's light laughter broke the tension as he opened the imaginary door and swaggered arrogantly across the white chalk line, reaching in the right-hand side of the cabinet to retrieve a matching mug to Shannon's. Pouring his coffee, he turned back to the table, pulled out the chair directly opposite her, and settled his long, lean frame in it comfortably.

"That's better," he observed lightheartedly, watching Shannon's radiant face come alive with amusement.

Shannon's smile faded slowly as her soft brown eyes met his dazzling sky-blue ones. "I'm sorry. I've been very rude and I know it."

Mitch picked up his coffee cup and took a taste of the hot liquid. "Don't worry about it," he dismissed lightly. "Let's just call a truce between us and get busy with running this place. From what I can tell, it's going to take all the energy we possess, without wasting time on childish bickering—agreed?"

"Agreed," Shannon acknowledged defeatedly. They were going to have to get along at least for a while.

"All right. Now, how have have you been, really?" he asked gently.

"I'm doing okay," she said softly, amazed at the way she could lie so convincingly to him. "How are you?"

He shrugged his broad shoulders indifferently. "The business is growing."

Shannon smiled tenderly. "I've heard a lot of good things about you."

His firm's name was becoming well known as one of the top builders in the steel industry. He was carrying on his father's name proudly.

"You really aren't seeing anyone seriously yet?" he questioned as he picked up his coffee cup again.

"No . . . no one seriously," she answered vaguely. "What about you?"

"No, I haven't been seeing anyone. I've been too

busy." He toyed with the spoon lying on the table. The silence seemed to stretch out uncomfortably.

"How's the . . . building coming along?"

"On schedule. Another six months will see it finished."

Shannon's eyes were fastened on her coffee cup. She really didn't know of anything impersonal to discuss with him, and she certainly didn't want the conversation to revert to a personal topic.

Mitch tossed the spoon back on the table and looked at her. "How have you really been, Shannon?"

"I've been fine, Mitch. I told you that."

"I meant it when I said I haven't seen you since the divorce. Not even a glimpse of you."

"St. Louis is a big city." Shannon shrugged her shoulders.

"What did you do about the apartment?"

"When the lease was up . . . I moved. I didn't need that much room."

"That's a shame. That was a nice apartment." Mitch's eyes stared out the window at the bright sunshiny morning.

"Yes, it was," she answered softly. It had nearly broken her heart to give it up, but she had seen Mitch in every room for months after their separation.

"I suppose you went back to work full time?"

"Yes, and I'm really enjoying it."

"You didn't need to," he reminded sharply. "I send you more than enough money to live on."

"I'm aware of that!" He had been more than generous, sending her above the agreed amount of alimony each month. "I wanted to go back to work."

"You should be home raising kids," he replied in a taut voice, "instead of sitting behind a desk all day."

"I don't *sit* behind a desk all day, and what I do with my life is my business! You should be married to have children . . . and I don't need to remind you, I'm not!"

"You could be! I don't need to remind *you* it wasn't *me* who wanted the divorce," he said angrily.

"You were given a choice between me, or your job. The job won," Shannon replied calmly.

Mitch leaned closer to her, his blue eyes intense. "I've told you a hundred times, I would give up that job as soon as the building was finished. I never planned to go back on my promise. You know that!"

"The only thing I know is that you did not love me enough to get someone else to do the job. You put the building ahead of *me* and our future."

"I can't understand how you can think that way! There are some things in life a man feels he has to do, Shannon, and finishing this project for Dad is one of them. It had nothing to do with my love for you. You always came first in my life, and you always would have if you would have only hung in there. . . ."

Shannon made herself look away from his pleading gaze. "I couldn't take the pressure . . . the worry . . . not every day, Mitch. I made your life miserable, and you sure made mine the same. You may very well have every intention of giving up working five hundred and fifty feet in the air every day, but in your case, there may never be a future."

"I'm not saying that couldn't happen, Shannon, but" —his voice dropped in a low husky timbre—"couldn't we have made the best of what time we had together? No one knows what tomorrow will bring. I could catch a cold and die of pneumonia today! Do you want me to

39

lock myself in some room and never come out simply because you're afraid of what could happen?"

"It's not the same, and you know it. You are deliberately flirting with death every day."

He grinned boyishly. "It could have been worse. I could have been flirting with women every day. But you know I never did that. I loved you too much ever to look at another woman. You should be thankful for that," he reasoned.

Shannon looked at him in disbelief. "Thankful! At least if you flirted with another woman, I could have boxed your ears and you would have been around to feel it!"

"Okay, okay! We had better drop the subject before we get into another damn shouting match!" Mitch got up and reached for the coffeepot. "I don't know how we ended up talking about the whole mess again in the first place," he mumbled more to himself than to her.

"You're the one who keeps bringing it up," she reminded him serenely. *"I* am trying my best to forget the past!"

"You're not the only one who doesn't want to relive the past," he snapped, pouring himself another cup of coffee. "It's taken me awhile, but, damn it, I think I'm finally over you!"

"I'm so happy for you!" she grumbled.

Mitch sat back down. "What?"

"I said, I'm very happy for you," Shannon repeated impatiently as she rose to take her cup to the sink. "Since we both agree we can live without each other, we apparently won't have any trouble being completely detached from each other while we are forced to work together the next few weeks."

"It won't bother me one bit," he agreed. "Do you want to ride to the hospital with me, or would you rather take your own car?"

"There's no need to take two cars," she answered in a professional tone. "I'll ride with you . . . if you don't mind."

"The car's heading in that direction. I don't care who rides in it."

"Well, you know me, I'm a sucker for sweet words." Shannon glared at him.

"Would you like for me to run down to the printers and have the invitation engraved on an embossed piece of paper for you?" He glared back at her.

"If you'll excuse me, I'll get dressed," she returned coolly, walking toward the door.

"I'm trying to 'excuse' you, but I must admit, it's getting harder all the time." He smiled sweetly.

Shannon whirled back around angrily.

"But, take your time," Mitch added, seeing the fire in her eyes. "I'm in no hurry!"

"Don't worry, I plan to."

"Oh, Shannon," Mitch called softly as she left the room.

"Yes?" She paused and turned around to face him.

"While we're around Jerry and Marla, we are going to put aside our differences. Now is not the time to carry on a war. You know how they used to worry about . . . things. I don't want them to think of anything except getting well. Don't you agree?"

"I agree completely."

"Good. Now, go get dressed. We have a tough day ahead of us." Mitch watched his ex-wife leave the room with a look of sadness in his eyes.

She was the one thing in his life he wished could have worked out differently. With a tired shrug he reached for his coffee cup. There'll be another woman, he consoled. There's *always* another woman.

CHAPTER THREE

The drive to the hospital took a little over thirty minutes from the resort. Mitch pulled up in front of the hospital that sat on top of a hill overlooking the town a little before noon. The small resort town was alive with activity this time of year. People from all over the United States flocked here each summer to visit the famed Silver Dollar City, Shepherd of the Hills pageant, as well as the numerous country music shows that lined Highway 76. Down in the tourist town itself, beautiful Lake Taneycomo lined its shores with avid trout fishermen camping in every available spot. "Pirate Cruises" ran hourly up and down the scenic lake.

Mitch found a parking place close to the front door. They both left the car, silently strolling toward the entrance of the hospital. Mitch took her arm and courteously ushered her inside. Her pulse pounded erratically at the touch of his hand on her bare arm.

As they entered the hushed atmosphere, Shannon was acutely aware of the distinct smell of medicine and sickness so common to hospitals. Mitch walked toward the elevator and pushed the up button as Shannon stood quietly beside him. The door slid silently open. Shannon stepped in first, with Mitch following and reaching around her to press the button for the second floor, his hand still holding her arm lightly. She could smell the faint aroma of his after-shave as the door closed, and her stomach came up in her throat as the elevator lifted them swiftly to the next floor. Sliding to a smooth halt, its large shiny doors slid back open noiselessly as they stepped out on the second floor.

"They're both still in intensive care," Mitch told her, walking down the small antiseptic hall. "Marla's on one side of the room, and Jerry's on the other. We'll see her first." He glanced to see if that was agreeable to Shannon.

Shannon nodded mutely, a sick feeling growing in the pit of her stomach.

Stopping before the double doors, Mitch's arm slipped casually down around her small waist. He looked down at her in concern. "You going to make it all right?"

Shannon nodded again soundlessly, taking a deep breath before entering the room. Her mind rebelled instantly as she let out a small audible gasp, her body tensing as her eyes focused on the small mound in the middle of the narrow hospital bed. Mitch's arm tightened perceptibly, pulling Shannon closer to his firm, comforting body. A nurse looked up from her desk and smiled reassuringly.

"I think Marla's awake, Mr. Wranebow. She's been wondering about you," she said. "Go right on over."

"Thanks." Mitch steered Shannon over to her sister's bedside.

Marla opened her eyes, tears forming in their hazel depths when she saw Shannon standing beside the bed. "Oh, Shannon," she whispered past swollen blue lips. "I thought you'd never get here."

Shannon let her tears flow freely now, as she leaned over carefully, enfolding Marla in her arms.

"I came as soon as I could," she assured her sister gently. "Everything will be fine, Marla. You're doing fine —really." Her tears mingled with her sister's.

A frightened sob caught in Marla's throat. "Oh, I hope so. I've been so frightened. I want to see Jerry," she pleaded, desperately clinging to Shannon's trembling hand.

"Jerry's on the other side of the room," Mitch reminded her tenderly, stepping up to stand beside Shannon. "The doctor said you two should be out of intensive care in another twenty-four to forty-eight hours. They plan on putting you both in the same room then," he comforted.

"Really?" Marla asked, her eyes lightening up with renewed hope.

"Would I kid my favorite sister-in-law?" Mitch teased. "But I'll bet in two weeks you'll be begging me and 'Bright Eyes' here to get Jerry a private room—away from you."

"Bright Eyes?" Marla looked from Shannon to Mitch questioningly. "It's been a long time since I've heard you call my sister that," she said hopefully.

"It's been a long time since I've seen her," Mitch said quietly.

A worried frown crossed Marla's face. "Oh, I hope you two can get along together for a while."

"Strike that thought from your pretty little head," Mitch encouraged Marla firmly. "Shannon's already told me how irresistible I am to her." He winked mischievously, leaning over to give an astounded Shannon a light kiss on her gaping mouth.

Shannon tensed. Bolts of brown lightning shot out of her eyes as she said in a tightly controlled voice, "Yes,

Marla, Mitch and I have decided to bury the hatchet for the time being." Right between his eyes, if he fools with me, she added silently.

"Good." Marla sighed weakly. "I was afraid you two would fight like cats and dogs," she confessed. "I'm sorry about your accommodations. Ever since Mitch mentioned that you and he would run the resort, I've been worried about where you both could stay, but there just doesn't seem to be any alternative, other than staying at our house."

Shannon's eyes let Mitch know she didn't appreciate him committing her before he had even discussed the matter with her.

"I'm concerned too about what our neighbors and summer guests will say about the arrangements," Marla continued, looking pointedly at Mitch and Shannon.

"It's none of their business," Shannon stated bluntly. "Good heavens, we were married!"

"Oh, I know," Marla agreed readily, "but you *are* divorced now. Of course, our neighbors and guests don't know that. . . . We run a family resort. . . ."

"You're not to worry about anything," Shannon consoled quietly. "Mitch and I will take over until you and Jerry get well, and we won't disgrace the family name."

"We can never repay you for what you're doing," Marla said weakly. "I know how hard this must be on both of you, but I love you, and we'll be eternally grateful."

"You'd both do the same for us," Shannon said lovingly. "I can force myself to stay with Mitch a few weeks."

Mitch's eyebrows rose sarcastically. "Force yourself?

That's really big of you, Shannon!" he said, disgust written clearly on his face.

"Well, I was just thinking," Marla piped back up quickly, seeing the black storm clouds gathering around Shannon's head. "Do you think you could just sort of *imply* that you were still married, so the neigh—"

"That would be totally stupid, Marla," Shannon blurted angrily. "I'm not going to put on an act—"

"Shannon," Mitch gritted out.

"Now, wait—listen, you two," Marla said, intervening in their growing spat. "I just meant, it would look better for the business and to our guests if you could just let *them* assume you're happily married. You wouldn't have to actually say you were! Now, don't you agree, Shannon?"

Shannon avoided looking directly at Mitch. "I'm afraid if anyone has the gall to ask, I'll tell them the truth!"

Mitch let out a scathing expletive under his breath as he turned away to face the window.

"Shannon!" Marla said in a low voice. "Try to control your temper and get along with Mitch. Please do this for Jerry and me. You came this far, please help us keep this business intact and reputable," she pleaded, her hazel eyes filling with tears again.

Shannon's heart fell to the floor. She was trapped. She was going to be suckered into this, and she couldn't stop it.

"All right," she relented slowly, "for you I'll do it, but only in public. In private we are totally divorced!"

"Oh, thank you, Shannon," Marla said gratefully. "I knew I could count on you—and, thank you, Mitch. I know what an imposition it is on you to leave your business and for Shannon to leave her job for so many weeks."

Mitch turned back from the window, his eyes boldly meeting Shannon's as he answered Marla. "You know we'd both do anything for you and Jerry. My men can handle things in St. Louis for a while. For right now, though, I think you've had more excitement than you need for one day," he said, his eyes taking in the gray pallor settling over her face. "We'll go over and see how Jerry is doing now and let you rest."

"Yes, I suppose you're right," Marla agreed in a tired voice. "Tell Jerry I love him, will you, Mitch?"

"Yes, but I refuse to kiss him for you," he teased affectionately.

Marla giggled weakly as Shannon leaned down to give her a good-bye hug.

"I'll bring you some pretty gowns when I come tomorrow," she promised.

"Thank you. I love you very much."

"I love you, too."

"What about me?" Mitch grinned cockily at the two sisters.

"Oh, I love you, too," Marla responded sincerely, while Shannon discreetly stomped on his foot as she left Marla's bedside.

"Damn it, Shannon!" he exploded under his breath. "Can't you take a joke?"

They stepped over to the far side of the room to visit with Jerry, staying only a few minutes when they saw how uncomfortable he was. His left leg was in a cast with numerous IV bottles dripping through needles in his arms; his face was covered with stitches, and he lay very pale and still on the narrow white hospital bed.

Mitch leaned down and spoke softly, giving Jerry Marla's love. Jerry nodded in silent agreement. It was far too painful to speak through the tube that was down his throat.

Shannon stepped over to the bed, taking one of his bruised hands in hers. "Hi, tough guy," she whispered tenderly. "Are you doing okay?"

Jerry managed a weak smile and lovingly squeezed her hand. Shannon's heart nearly broke to see these two people whom she dearly loved so broken and helpless.

Promising to return the next day, Mitch and Shannon left the hospital, making the return trip home in silence, each one deep in their own troubled thoughts.

Mitch let them back into the house with his key, going immediately to his side of the room. He stood for a moment looking out at the sparkling lake. "I thought we had called a truce. What the hell were you trying to prove awhile ago at the hospital?" he asked tensely.

"We did, but I refuse to be a hypocrite and pose as a happily married couple when we're not!"

Mitch expelled a tired sigh of resignation. "Have it your way, Shannon, when we're alone, but I told you when we're around Marla and Jerry you're going to play your part, damn it! I don't want them worrying over our problems along with their own," he said angrily.

Shannon shrugged her shoulders in total rejection of his statement and started to walk past him to her bedroom. "Sorry, but I don't take orders from you anymore," she said coolly.

With lightning swiftness, Mitch reached out and jerked her roughly to a sudden halt. She caught her breath in surprise as he brought his face down close to hers and threatened sternly. "Listen, lady, I didn't ask you for that

49

damn divorce, nor did I want it! But since you insisted on going through with it, I want you to get one thing straight. In the future when I'm talking to you, don't you *ever* turn around and walk out on me. For the next few weeks you're going to listen to what I say whether you like it or not!"

Shannon's legs turned traitorously weak as the very familiar smell of him assailed her senses. Her eyes closed for a minute, her insides turning to mush as she leaned against him, her arms unwillingly reaching up to encircle his neck.

A brief look of surprise crossed his features at her response, his voice growing more gentle. He pulled her up tighter between his taut thighs, making her aware of the difference between a man and a woman. "You keep pushing me on this, and you'll make the next few weeks nothing but misery," he said in an unsteady timbre. One long finger reached out to gently trace the outline of her face, his blue eyes savoring its creamy perfection.

Shannon could barely think now as he moved suggestively up against her, pressing her to him tightly. Where was all her newfound independence, her unwavering resolve to forget him? She was turning to putty once more in his familiar embrace.

"Let me go, Mitch," she ordered, finally able to find her voice. "I don't know what got into me. . . ." Her voice trailed off pitifully as she saw his mouth descending to meet hers.

"Just shut up, damn it. I'm going to kiss you whether you like it or not!" His mouth touched hers lightly, his breathing growing heavier as his hands moved exploringly down her back, sending cold shivers of delight coursing wildly through her trembling body. She should not be standing here letting him do what he was doing, and she had every intention of stopping him in just a few more minutes. . . .

"Mitch, please," she whispered against his insistent mouth. "We shouldn't be doing this. . . ." Shannon had gone limp in his arms now, all reason and control evaporating with the touch of his hands coming up to cup her breasts, his fingers leisurely stroking the small buds into tautness.

"Are you going to deny you want this as much as I do?" His breath mingled with hers sweetly, their tongues reaching out to touch each other's seductively.

"Come here, Bright Eyes. It's been a long time. . . ." Mitch groaned, capturing her mouth roughly, his tongue plunging deeply into the warm recesses of her mouth. A searing shaft of desire tightened within her as memories of Mitch and her making love ran rampant in her confused mind. It had always been like some unexplainable, crazy magic when they were together. He could take her to paradise and keep her there for hours with the very greatest of ease. Once again he was weaving his deadly spell on her as his hands stroked and caressed her, his mouth hungrily making up for all the months they had been apart. She heard him moan low and painfully as he reached to unsnap her jeans and slip his hand down the front, his fingers touching her intimately.

"No. *No!*" she panted, jerking out of his demanding embrace. "I told you I would *not* let this happen."

"Oh, good grief, Shannon," he pleaded hoarsely, "don't do this. You know how good it can be between us. Surely you want me," he pleaded, reaching out to pull her back into his arms, his eyes burning with desire for her.

51

She backed away from him in frightened terror. How could she have let things get out of hand? He didn't love her anymore. He only wanted her in his bed again. He had told her he was more than happy the divorce was final.

"Stay away from me, Mitch! I warn you, I won't stay here with you if this ever happens again!" she threatened in a shaky voice. "Just leave me *alone!*"

Mitch's face had grown angrier with each word, his temper boiling over now. "Oh, I'll leave you alone, Shannon. I could tell you were hating every moment of that kiss!" he shouted heatedly.

Shannon spun around on her heel, heading for the sanctity of her bedroom, her temper matching his now. "And don't you speak to me again without knocking! Do you understand?" she screeched as she marched angrily toward her bedroom.

"You stubborn . . ." Mitch stomped over to the couch, fighting to bring his killer instinct under control. "I wouldn't knock on your damn door if my side of the room was burning to the ground!" he yelled back defiantly.

"Good! I'd probably throw your rear right back into the fire, you . . . you . . . demented sex maniac!" she retaliated as she slammed her bedroom door.

That man was going to drive her up a wall! She fell across her bed, beating the pillows in extreme frustration. If he thought for one minute she was going to fall back into his bed like a lovesick schoolgirl, he had another think coming! She had her pride! If he didn't want the divorce, he could have begged her forgiveness, given up his profession . . . but he hadn't done that. He had let her know he was his own man and he would not let her decide his occupation. No, all he wanted was a tumble in the hay to while away his hours until he got back to the big city! Well, he was out of luck! She would not become involved with him again!

The upsetting emotions of the past day and a half took their toll on her as Shannon slipped into a fatigued sound sleep, casting all her cares aside in the black inky void of unconsciousness. It was late afternoon when she awakened, feeling almost like her old self again. She lay for a moment listening for any sounds from the other part of the house. Her mind drifted lazily back over the argument that had erupted between her and Mitch earlier. They couldn't seem to be in the same room together without their tempers flaring, and for the life of her, she didn't know why. He was the one person she loved the most in her life, but she was determined he would be kept in the dark on that little fact!

Noting by the clock on her bedside stand that it was nearly dinner time, she rose slowly and walked into the bathroom. After washing her face, she brushed her hair vigorously, trying to restore some order to the curly locks.

As she walked back to the kitchen, the telephone on the wall reminded her she had better call her office and let Molly know that she was going to have to be gone at least a month or longer. Luckily, she would be able to take the time off. Molly could keep things running smoothly for a few weeks, and her boss, Mr. Dyer, would undoubtedly understand the emergency situation. As she dialed the number, she glanced out the window wondering who the tall nice-looking man was that Mitch was talking to. The handsome blond stranger was pointing out different areas around the resort, gesturing animatedly with his hands.

After clearing things with her office, she hung up the phone and walked over to the cabinet to get a large glass. She made iced tea and was just sitting down to drink it when the front door opened and Mitch stepped in with the stranger.

"Shannon?" Mitch looked surprised to see her there. "I didn't think you were awake yet."

"I just woke up." Shannon looked at him suspiciously. "How did you know I was asleep?"

Mitch grinned uncomfortably. "When I didn't hear you beating your pillow anymore, I opened your door a fraction to check on you." Turning to the man standing next to him, who was eyeing Shannon appreciatively, he continued. "This is Cliff Webster. He's been looking after this place until we arrived to take over."

Shannon smiled pleasantly as Cliff stepped forward and took her hand, squeezing it intimately. "Shannon, I've heard a lot about you from Marla. She always said you were better-looking than her, but I thought she had to be joking! I can see I was wrong!" His eyes boldly skipped over her feminine curves, coming to rest casually on the cleft in her plunging neckline. "I understand you're a divorcée," he added lightly.

A brief glance at Mitch laid her fear to rest that he had been the one to give Cliff that information. His face was rigid in a tight mask, his cold blue eyes resting on her hand that was being gripped tightly by another man.

"Who told you that?" Mitch snapped.

"Why, Marla did." Cliff turned around to face Mitch. "Oh, goodness! Are *you* the ex-husband? Trust me to stick my foot in my mouth," he exclaimed embarrassedly.

"Don't let it bother you; she *is* a divorcée," Mitch said pointedly.

"We have decided to try to keep the divorce as quiet as possible, Cliff," Shannon intervened quickly. "Marla and Jerry think that it would be better for the business if everyone assumed we were still married. They cater to families that come here year after year, and they don't want anyone feeling uncomfortable."

"Sure, I understand. There's a lot of people who would frown on you two living in the same house together. In a business like this you can't be too careful about those things," Cliff agreed readily. He grinned at her suggestively. "I was just asking for my own personal information."

Shannon withdrew her hand from his. Whatever surface attraction she had first experienced for him evaporated rapidly. He was entirely too assuming!

"Would you care for something cold to drink, Mr. Webster?" she asked politely. "I just made a pitcher of iced tea."

Smiling at her as if she had just invited him into her bedroom for the afternoon, he replied in a sexy tone, "Love some."

Shannon would have liked nothing better than to have slapped the smug look off of his face, but instead she turned toward Mitch and asked pleasantly, "Would you like a glass of iced tea, also?"

"I was just about to 'knock,' " he said snidely. "Will that be necessary?"

"Yes," Shannon spit back tersely, both of them forgetting about their company for the moment.

"All right," he said. "Knock-knock . . . dammit!" His heated blue eyes bore into hers challengingly.

"Why, Mr. Wranebow! Do come in," she gushed sweetly, feigning surprise, not the least bit intimidated by his belligerent manner.

Mitch opened the imaginary door and slammed it shut defiantly before he sat down at the table with a puzzled Cliff.

"What was that all about?" Cliff asked Mitch.

"You wouldn't believe me if I told you," Mitch grumbled, then hurriedly changed the subject. "Can you give me a quick rundown of what needs to be done to keep this place running on a day-to-day basis?" he asked.

"It's a big job this time of the year," Cliff warned. "Do either one of you know anything about running a tourist resort?"

Shannon carried the glasses of iced tea over to the table and sat down with the two men. "I'm afraid not," she answered lamely.

"Well, of course, I live about two miles from the resort and have my own job as administrator at the hospital Jerry and Marla are in, but I'll be around if you need any help." He looked at Shannon again, his eyes flashing her a hidden message. "And please don't hesitate to ask."

Mitch set his half-empty glass back down on the table loudly. "So, why don't you fill me in on what needs to be done, Cliff? We don't want to take up your time. I'm sure you have other things you need to be doing."

"Yes . . . well." He pulled his eyes away from Shannon. "There's grass to be mowed, Marla's vegetable garden to be taken care of, and you'll have to put the chemicals in the pool every day. Marla has two women that come in to help her clean the cottages and do the laundry every day. There's a couple of roofs that need repairing, and the hot water heater in cottage four went on the blink yesterday—plus a hundred smaller repairs that need to be made. Most of the twenty cottages are rented at the moment," he droned on, then stopped suddenly. "By the way, Mitch, wait till you get a load of the redheaded bombshell in cottage nine." Cliff let out a low suggestive whistle as he drew a figure of a curvaceous woman in midair. "If you're looking for any action . . ."

"I'm not looking for any action, Cliff," Mitch said irritably. "Is there anything else we need to know?"

"Oh, there'll be something new every day. A place like this is nothing but a pain in the . . ." he stopped, glancing at Shannon briefly. "Well, let's just say you'll both have your hands full. But, as I said, I'll be around." His eyes rested on Shannon once more.

"Thanks for looking after things, Cliff." Mitch stood up, offering him his hand. "We'll call you if we need anything." Cliff was being dismissed in a curt, professional business tone, and before he knew what was happening, he was being ushered out the back door.

As the screen slammed shut, Mitch turned back to Shannon, his face set in a determined, stony mask. "I don't plan on telling you this but once, Shannon. I don't intend to get in another verbal battle, but I just want to make you aware of a few rules of my own, starting right now. That Webster is nothing but trouble, and I don't want you around him any more than necessary." Shannon was amazed at the tranquil way Mitch was speaking, his voice never rising beyond a normal level. "It's true, we are divorced, but at the moment we have Jerry and Marla's business at stake, and I don't plan on standing idly by while some fair-haired Romeo makes a pass at you. Is that perfectly clear?"

She knew by the tone of his voice he would brook no argument from her on this particular ultimatum. Not that he would have needed to have warned her about Cliff in the first place. Cliff Webster would be the *last* man to warrant even a second thought from her. "I understand," she replied softly.

"Good." He turned and started to walk to his side of the house, pausing as another thought surfaced. "One more thing, Shannon."

Shannon glanced back up in surprise. "Yes?"

"Just in case you get to wondering. I have *no* intentions of checking out the 'bombshell' in cottage nine . . . or ten . . . or twelve . . . or whatever damn cottage some good-looking broad may be staying in. As I said earlier, as far as *I'm* concerned, at the moment . . . we are still married. I'm not on the make for another woman." His mouth was drawn in a taut line, his eyes turning a dark, angry blue. "Is that clear?"

"Yes."

"I know what was between us is dead and buried," he said huskily, "and for the life of me I don't know why I find it necessary to say this, but for some stupid unexplained reason it's important to me for you to hear it." His tone grew softer now. "For what it's worth, Bright Eyes, I haven't looked at, touched, thought about, and damn sure never went to bed with another woman since we separated." His stony mask of composure broke as he turned and strode impatiently toward his bedroom. The sound of the door closing shattered the silence in the quiet kitchen and the cool composure of the girl sitting alone.

"Thank you," Shannon murmured, so softly that no one else could hear her. "I haven't either."

Tears dotted Marla's tablecloth as Shannon watched the widening circles of wetness grow in front of her. How was it possible to feel the pain she was experiencing right now? She had thought that all the hurt was behind her now, foolishly believing that she would eventually be able to forget Mitchell Wranebow! But suddenly, here she was, right back where she started, with only the future without him looming bleakly ahead of her.

CHAPTER FOUR

The following days flew by swiftly, with daily trips to the hospital to see Marla and Jerry, and the effort to familiarize themselves with the resort and their new responsibilities. Shannon and Mitch had managed to be civil to each other, but just barely.

When they had returned home from the hospital the first day, they had sat down over dinner and tried to assess what were the most pressing items to be taken care of. They had found to their astonishment that there was enough work to keep ten people busy for the next several months. One guest had come to the door, badly in need of someone to take care of a faulty hot water heater, and one had come to tell them that there was a leak in the roof, discovered after the heavy rain of the night before.

Several wanted clean linens and towels, one man pleaded with Mitch to tell him where the best fishing holes were, and an extremely obnoxious woman with three overbearing children wanted Shannon to baby-sit while she and her husband took in the local sights that night.

Mitch burst through the doorway in midafternoon of the second day, his face as white as a sheet.

"What in the world is the matter with you?" Shannon

60

asked, turning from her task of folding a huge mound of bed linens she had just taken off the line.

"This place is a madhouse!" Mitch exclaimed in an exasperated voice. "A Doberman just tried to take a bite out of my leg! I'd much rather be crawling around on beams hundreds of feet in the air any day of the week!"

Shannon ignored the reference to his preference and slumped tiredly down in a chair at the kitchen table.

"The work here is a big change from what we're used to doing," she agreed. "Would you like something cold to drink?"

Mitch glanced up, surprised that she would offer her services to him. As a rule she wouldn't give him the time of day if he asked. "Yeah, I'd love something cold to drink," he responded gratefully.

Shannon rose and went to the cabinet, taking out two glasses and filling them with ice. In a few moments she walked to the chalk line and handed him his glass of iced tea politely.

"Thanks!" he grunted, taking a large swallow from the frosty glass.

Shannon returned to her seat and took a sip of her drink, quietly contemplating the seemingly endless chores still awaiting her.

"Did you get a good look at that flower garden?" Mitch asked glumly.

Shannon nodded. "And have you seen that humongous vegetable garden Marla has planted?"

Mitch nodded bleakly.

"Well," Shannon sighed, "it's going to be up to us to take care of them."

Mitch finished his cold drink in one large swallow before rising slowly to his feet. "Let's go out and take a closer look at them," he suggested resignedly.

Shannon trailed Mitch as they stepped out the back door. With the thermometer hovering around one hundred degrees, it felt as if they had stepped into a blast furnace. With determined strides Mitch led them to the large flower garden, which was fast becoming overgrown with weeds.

They both stood staring at the object in question.

"Well, what do you think?" Shannon asked.

"I think someone would have to be nuts to plant one of these things," he observed irritably.

"Do you know anything about taking care of flowers?" Shannon asked hopefully.

Mitch glanced at her sharply. "Do I look like I know anything about flowers?"

"Well, I certainly don't," she affirmed. "I'm the only person alive that can walk into a room filled with flowers, and they immediately start to wilt!"

Mitch shook his head. "What about vegetable gardens? You know anything about taking care of one of those?"

"Not really," Shannon admitted.

"I thought women were supposed to know all about these kinds of things!"

"Congratulations, you've just met a woman who doesn't." She smiled sarcastically.

"You're going to be a big help!" he grumbled, shoving his hand in the pocket of his trousers.

"Look. I didn't plant these stupid gardens, but they're here! If you'll take care of this one, I'll see what I can do about all those millions of green beans and tomatoes hanging on the vines in the vegetable garden," she bargained.

62

"That's fine with me! I don't know poo-diddley about either one of them!"

"Just great! We should make a humdinger of a team." Shannon turned on her heel, heading for the storage shed where Marla had said that Jerry kept the garden tools and lawn mower. "You are aware that we also have acres of grass to mow in addition to our other gardening responsibilities," she said crossly as she opened the door to the shed. "Do you at least know how to do that?"

"Yes, I know how to do that!" he mimicked nastily. "I don't know why you're getting so hot under the collar! Of course, I know how to mow the grass! But, you're getting all bent out of shape just because I don't know how to work in some damn lousy"—he gestured wildly at the flower bed sitting forlornly out in the blistering sun— "pansy garden!"

"Shhh . . . keep your voice down," she hissed sharply. "The guests will think we're crazy!"

"Well, they wouldn't be far off . . . in regards to one of us!" he mumbled under his breath as he scooped up a hoe and shovel. "If you'll excuse me, Ms. Murphy," he stressed her maiden name tersely, "I have work to do." He stalked off regally in the direction of his assigned flower bed.

Shannon noticed that the back of his shirt was already soaked with perspiration from the humidity of the day. A small smile crept over her features as she watched him marching angrily to his assignment. Lawn work had never been one of his favorite things. When they were married, they had lived in an apartment complex where the lawn work was taken care of by hired personnel. Oh, well, she shrugged, it certainly wasn't one of her favorite things either, but the gardens and the lawn had to be taken care of.

For the next few days they both worked diligently at trying to restore some semblance of order to the two gardens. Combined with the other backbreaking chores of the resort, they were both near exhaustion each night. Mitch stayed well behind his chalk line, and Shannon stayed behind hers. Their meals were the same thing every day. Mitch had a jar of peanut butter, a jar of jelly, and a loaf of white bread he kept by his chair in the living room. Since Shannon was stuck with the kitchen and her bedroom as her part of the house, she always sat at the kitchen table eating her bowls of cold cereal, steadfastly refusing to even glance in the direction of the living room. Not once in the four days they had been together had she invited him to join her, except for the first morning when they had shared coffee together and that night when they had discussed the situation over dinner.

The refrigerator and counter tops were overflowing with tomatoes and green beans, leaving very little room for groceries, which neither Mitch nor Shannon had the time nor the energy to shop for.

On the morning of the fifth day they had eaten their scanty breakfast, then hurried out to work on the gardens before the heat became unbearable.

Shannon picked the tomatoes and green beans, then took them into the house to try to find room for them on the counter tops. She was going to have to do something before long, or most of Marla's crops were going to rot.

Mitch came bounding in the back door an hour later, proudly announcing that the flower garden was now back to normal. He ushered Shannon out the door, beaming with pride as he showed her a flourishing summer flower garden, its colors blooming vividly in the sunlight. The garden was now void of even the slightest sign of a weed.

"What do you think of that?" he asked with a grin.

Shannon eyed the garden critically, but failed to find one thing in error. "It looks very nice," she admitted.

"Well, it was one hell of a job, but I must admit it looks perfect now!"

"I don't know that I'd classify it as 'perfect,' but it does look better," Shannon granted graciously.

Mitch looked at her and grinned. "You're just mad because yours doesn't look as good."

"I am not. Mine looks every bit as good as yours does!" They both knew that was a lie.

"Whatever you say," he dismissed airily, "but you've got to admit mine looks a heck of a lot better than it did three days ago."

Relenting somewhat, Shannon gave him a polite smile. "I'll admit that."

"Come on, Shannon, can't you do just a little better than that?" he coaxed in a teasing tone. "After all, this is the first real piece of evidence we've had that all this hard work we've been doing is going to pay off."

"Oh, Mitch, I am proud of you," she relented, giving him a broad, friendly grin. "It does look lovely!"

"I know." He grinned back. "You want me to help you whip that vegetable garden into shape?"

Shannon's grin faded. "No, I don't! I can hold up my end of the bargain."

"Just thought I'd offer," he defended himself. "Personally, I'm getting tired of keeping company with green beans and tomatoes."

"I plan on canning all those vegetables," she said coolly.

"Canning them? Are you serious? You don't know how to can."

"I can learn, can't I? Besides, Marla says it's easy. All I have to do is wash them, put them in the jars, then into the pressure cooker. What could be simpler than that?"

Mitch looked skeptical. "I've heard of those pressure cookers exploding," he warned.

Shannon grunted disgustedly. "How ridiculous! I'm not a complete idiot, Mitch."

"Maybe not complete, but I still want you to warn me when you start your home canning project."

Two days later Shannon had no choice but to try her hand at home canning. There was no longer any room in the kitchen for even one more green bean.

She decided to strip the linens off her bed, then do her share of the mowing in the morning. By the afternoon, barring any unforeseen emergencies, she would have time to tackle the canning.

Mitch had walked out the door earlier, trying to gag down another peanut butter sandwich. He didn't seem in too good of a mood this morning, since he didn't give his perfunctory "knock-knock" as he walked by her. For one split second she thought of taking pity on him and at least changing the sheets on his bed, but that passed swiftly. He could change his own. He certainly wasn't taking any pity on her. Other than his one offer to help in the garden, he had politely let her do her share of the work—and more, it seemed to Shannon.

She could hear the mower running as she dusted in her bedroom and put new sheets on her bed. Thirty minutes later she was pouring herself a second cup of coffee when she heard the mower fall silent. Stepping over to look out the window, a nagging sense of jealousy erupted as she saw the redheaded divorcée who was staying in cottage nine. She was dressed in a brief bikini, leaning seductively toward Mitch. Shannon seethed as she watched her ex-husband sitting on the riding lawn mower, happily chattering away with the nearly nude bombshell.

The hot sun was glistening off his bare, muscular chest, which was shiny from sweat in the morning heat. The white pair of tennis shorts he was wearing could only call attention to how well he was built, a fact that Shannon was trying very hard to ignore lately.

Shannon had stiffened as Rhonda Neilson laughed flirtatiously at something Mitch had just said to her. So much for his promise that he wasn't looking for any action!

Mitch's laugh rang out again, and Shannon watched miserably as his white teeth and flirting blue eyes were turned on Rhonda.

Slamming her coffee cup down on the table heatedly, she rushed to his bedroom and angrily took one of his T-shirts out of his top drawer. Rushing back through the living room, she slowed her pace down so that when she actually stepped out the door and walked toward the chattering couple, she looked very cool, calm, and collected. A far cry from what she actually felt!

Strolling up casually to them, she threw the T-shirt in his surprised face, and snapped, "Put this on! It's much too hot out here in the sun to mow without your shirt on . . . darling," she added in an afterthought for Rhonda's benefit. As far as the guests were concerned, Mitch and Shannon had put on the appearance of a happily married couple . . . at least a couple who were married.

Mitch glanced up in disbelief. "Why in the world

67

would I want to put a shirt on? It must be a hundred in the shade right now."

"I just told you! You'll burn up without your shirt on," Shannon reasoned crossly.

A knowing smile crept across Mitch's handsome features. "Oh, why of course . . . darling. How thoughtful of you to care about my comfort," he drawled lovingly.

"Good morning, Mrs. Neilson." Shannon smiled, ignoring Mitch's taunting grin. "It sure is hot, isn't it?"

"Ms. Neilson, and, yes, it is rather warm," Rhonda corrected with what Shannon viewed as a most insincere smile.

"My, my, this does feel better," Mitch remarked, trying to slip the cotton shirt over his sticky, sweaty chest. "I can't understand why I didn't think of it earlier!" He grinned at Shannon affectionately. "Now all I need is a cup of hot tea and I'll be in hog heaven."

Shannon put a possessive arm around Mitch, smiling a silent warning to the redhead. "I hope you're enjoying your stay here, Ms. Neilson, and if you should need anything, be sure and let *me* know," she stressed. "My husband usually has his hands full."

"She's right." Mitch pulled Shannon closer, shooting her a mocking glare. "My sweet little wife keeps me busy day *and* night, but do feel free to call on *either* one of us, if you need anything."

Rhonda eyed Mitch's muscular physique longingly. "Why thank you, Mitchell. That's very kind of you." Her full, raspberry lips parted seductively in a sexy smile.

"I'll mow now, sweetheart," Shannon said, nearly knocking Mitch off the mower in her eagerness to break up the conversation. "You can get started on that leaky roof in cabin six."

"Now? As hot as it is?" Mitch's face was flushed a bright red from the heat and the warmth of the shirt he had been forced to put on.

"What better time?" Shannon scolded irritably. "It looks like rain to me, and the Mensons have a right to expect a dry cabin!"

Rhonda and Mitch both glanced up into the blue, cloudless sky, then back to Shannon quizzically.

"Do you know how to use this?" Mitch asked Shannon as he resignedly slid off the seat of the mower and watched her take his place.

"Of course, I know how to use a riding lawn mower," she snapped curtly, wishing that Ms. Rhonda Neilson would take a hint and shove off!

"Now, Shannon, this is not a toy," Mitch cautioned. "You can get yourself hurt real easy on a piece of machinery that you're not used to."

"I am perfectly able to take care of myself, Mitch," Shannon said coolly. "Kindly step out of my way so I can get started. I don't have all day, you know."

"Whatever you say, Muley." Mitch stepped back from the mower and bowed gallantly.

"Don't start with the Muley bit!" Shannon shot him a scathing look.

"Then don't act like one," Mitch said calmly. He knew that calling Shannon stubborn was like waving a red flag in front of a bull, so during their marriage he had discreetly started referring to her as Muley if she was showing a streak of stubbornness. "Now, are you *sure* you know how to operate this mower?"

"Positive! Now bug off . . . darling." Shannon smiled sweetly as she glanced toward a puzzled Rhonda.

Running a riding lawn mower could not be that hard,

she reasoned as she tried to remember what she should do first. On this particular mower, there was a hand lever for the gas and a pedal for the brake. That was all simple enough. Surely she could manage to get this thing to work!

Easing out on the gas lever slowly, she gave Mitch and Rhonda her most superior look as the mower purred smoothly by them, throwing grass systematically out the back side of the mower. Ha! Simple as falling off a log!

Shannon hummed along merrily on the mower, smug in the assurance that she was doing as good a job as *he* had done. She made three or four turns neatly, driving back and forth across the large yard in front of the cottages. There absolutely was nothing to this, she thought, picking up speed with each new turn. In another ten minutes she was flying along, throwing up a cloud of grass behind her like a Texas whirlwind. Perhaps she should slow down just a little, she thought a few minutes later as she once again had a bit of trouble coordinating the gas lever and the brake pedal.

Cautiously, she backed the mower around the side of cottage two, and lined it up with the narrow patch between the pool and the flower garden Mitch was so proud of. Eyeing the narrow patch skeptically, she shifted into forward. This was going to take a piece of tricky driving, but feeling more than confident, she pressed down on the gas lever and shot forward.

Boy, that Rhonda Neilson certainly didn't know how to take a hint, Shannon seethed irritably as she came back around cottage two and noticed that the pushy redhead had followed Mitch over to cottage six and was now holding the ladder as he climbed up to the blazing hot roof with a mouthful of nails and a large hammer stuffed carelessly in the waistband of his white shorts.

Cutting a large swath down the front of cottage two, Shannon headed for the narrow patch of ground that would require all her concentration. Her mower was picking up speed again as her eyes kept coming back to Mitch and Rhonda involuntarily. She hated to admit it, but their little intimate scene was bugging the devil out of her! That rotten Rhonda was a woman on the make if Shannon ever saw one! Not that it made any difference. Mitch was certainly free to pursue any woman he wanted, but Shannon felt it was rather tacky for her ex-husband to actively pursue someone right under her nose! After all, he had forbidden her to have anything to do with Cliff Webster, so why should *he* have access to a willing and eager redheaded divorcée!

The mower surged forward at an alarming rate, tossing grass wildly in the air.

"You'd better slow down, Shannon!" She heard Mitch shout above the roar of the mower.

Shannon cast him a look of exasperation as she pressed down harder on the gas lever, fighting the urge to shout childishly back at him to mind his own business. Rhonda must be getting a real laugh out of this!

For a moment it didn't register that Mitch was staring back at her now, until she saw the nails dropping systematically one by one out of his mouth.

What's his problem? she wondered, surprised by the look of terror on his face.

Suddenly Mitch came alive. He began jumping up and down on the roof, pointing in Shannon's direction, shouting at her at the top of his lungs.

"What?" Shannon shouted back crossly. Obviously she was doing something that had him upset.

"Watch where you're going!" he bellowed, gesturing wildly with both arms. "You're going to hit my flow—"

Shannon cringed, then grimaced, as the air suddenly came alive with flying dahlias, marigolds and irises. A large chunk of elephant-ears came shooting past her as the mower continued to plow through the large weed-free garden Mitch had worked so laboriously on for days. Jamming her foot on the brake pedal, she skidded the mower to a jarring halt.

Glancing back over her shoulder, Shannon gulped, her face turning bright red. Holy cow! There was a wide bald strip running right through the center of the flower garden several feet long.

Hazarding an uneasy glance in Mitch's direction, she moaned as she saw him sink dejectedly down on the sweltering roof, looking stunned as he surveyed the hundreds of pieces of shredded flowers scattered haphazardly over the yard.

Rhonda was standing next to the ladder, pieces of marigolds hanging off her perfectly coiffeured hair, her cool features watching Shannon. Hesitating only a moment, Shannon slithered guiltily off the mower, feeling like a total fool. An idea occurred to her from out of the blue as she started running toward Marla and Jerry's house, her eyes deliberately avoiding Mitch and Rhonda.

"Stay where you are, I'll get it!" she yelled as she ran faster for an imaginary ringing telephone.

Mitch and Rhonda watched speechlessly as Shannon streaked by them and rushed into the house, slamming the door behind her.

Leaning against the door of the cabin, Shannon let out

a relieved sigh. That was the most embarrassing thing that had ever happened to her! She walked over to the kitchen sink and wet a paper towel. Squeezing out the water, she ran it over her hot, flushed face. Wiping the strands of perspiration-soaked hair off her forehead, she almost started to cry. Mitch undoubtedly didn't think she was playing with a full deck, and right now, she might just agree she did have a couple of aces missing!

Her eyes once more were confronted with the mounds of vegetables lying on every available space in the kitchen. Shannon needed to keep busy so she could stay inside, and she had put it off long enough. Something was going to have to be done about those hateful things! For the following two hours, she worked diligently, putting the beans and tomatoes in the canning jars, then into the huge pressure cooker sitting on the stove. That was the part that tended to make her extremely nervous. Mitch's words of gloom and doom about the possibility of the pressure cooker blowing up came back to haunt her. Nonetheless, she worked steadily throughout the afternoon, and was successful. She was now slipping the last of the green bean jars into the cooker.

Glancing out the window, she saw that Mitch was standing on the side of the house talking to one of the male guests who was staying in cabin ten. Mitch had been in and out of the house periodically all afternoon, but he had said very little to Shannon. At least he hadn't mentioned his precious flower bed, and for that Shannon was grateful. The kitchen windows were wide open to let some of the heat escape from the kitchen, but it was still terribly warm in the house. The air-conditioning unit was not working properly, and as yet, Mitch hadn't found time to fix it.

A light tap on the front screen brought her attention back to the present as she recognized one of Marla's neighbors standing at the door.

"Cathy," Shannon greeted her happily, "come on in!" Shannon walked to the door and opened it to let her in. "It's terribly hot, isn't it?"

"It sure is. I thought you might want to have a glass of lemonade with me." Cathy held up two glasses of sparkling cold lemonade. "How about it?"

"It looks heavenly." Shannon reached out and gratefully accepted one of the extended glasses.

"Mitch said you were canning. How's it going?" Cathy asked as she followed Shannon out onto the front porch of the house. They both sank into the chaise longues with a grateful sigh. "You look like you've been digging ditches all afternoon," she observed with a friendly grin.

"I feel like I've been digging ditches," Shannon admitted. "Canning is hard work! I have the last of the jars in now. I don't see how Marla stands it."

Cathy's grin broadened. "You'll get used to it. How are Marla and Jerry today?"

"Doing better. I talked to Marla this morning. They both seem to be improving every day, but the doctor still thinks it will be close to Labor Day before either one of them can be released."

"Well, I'm just thankful they're progressing as well as they are. They both gave us a terrible scare. By the way, I think we are going to have a few people over next week for a cookout. Trev has promised to do all the cooking. Can you and Mitch make it?"

Shannon looked uneasy as she took another sip of her lemonade, debating whether to tell Cathy the truth concerning Mitch's and her relationship. Deciding that she

74

would rather not get into such a sticky discussion at the moment, she promised to ask Mitch if he thought they could spare the time away from the resort. Mentally she made a note to use that flimsy excuse when she called Cathy back to refuse the invitation.

"Try to make it," Cathy urged. "I want you to meet Brenda and Nathan Daniels. They're the neighbors on the other side of us. I don't think you've met them since you've been here, have you?"

Shannon shook her head.

"I didn't think so," Cathy said. "They were in Springfield for a couple of weeks visiting with their best friends, Price and Erin Seaver, who just had a new baby a month ago. If you ever want to hear a romantic story, have Brenda tell you about the Seavers. They met while baby-sitting for Brenda's twins and after a few weeks were married."

"Sounds romantic," Shannon agreed absently, silently thinking that those kinds of love stories rarely happened in real life. At least she hadn't ever been able to make them happen to her.

The women chatted on for another ten minutes or so before Cathy finally took notice of the time. "Oh, I've got to be going. Michael will be waking up from his nap anytime, and I haven't even thought about what to have for dinner. Trevor is a real bear if his dinner's late!" Cathy slid off the lounge and retrieved Shannon's empty glass. "Come over when you can, and be sure to ask Mitch about the cookout next week. Promise?"

Shannon laughed. "I promise."

"Good. I'll talk to you soon, and give my love to Marla and Jerry. I probably won't get by the hospital until one day next week."

"I'll tell her." Shannon watched Cathy scurry off in the direction of her home, a tugging sense of loneliness befalling her. For a moment she recalled all the plans she and Mitch had made for children and a new house when they were married. All those plans were nothing but cold, empty dreams now.

Wiping away the mist that had sprung to her eyes, she walked back into the house. She paused and listened intently to the loud, sputtering, hissing noise coming from the kitchen. What in the— She ran into the kitchen, her eyes focusing on the whistling, puffing pan. Peering suspiciously at the frantically bobbing cap, she mumbled aloud. "That's strange. It didn't sound like this earlier this afternoon."

Shannon's brown eyes grew decidedly larger as she started backing fearfully out of the kitchen, the cooker now sounding very much like a missile about to leave its launch pad.

She turned, intending to give the pan plenty of room to do its thing, when she heard a horrendous explosion that rocked the whole house. Green beans and tomatoes belched out into the air as the lid blew off the pressure cooker, sending it spiraling through the screen of the kitchen window.

Shannon was grabbing blindly for the handle on the front screen door when the door opened. A white-faced Mitch bolted inside, dodging the spewing green beans and trying to hold on to a terrified Shannon. His foot slipped on a thick layer of beans covering the floor as he grabbed for her and both of them went down on their knees, sliding halfway across the room before coming to a dead halt flat on their backs. Mitch was lying on top of Shannon, stunned as her arms came up around his neck to clasp him to her tightly. Her eyes were clamped shut as she squeezed harder, still not sure what had just taken place.

"Let go," he wheezed out weakly. "You're choking me!"

"What happened?" she asked as her grip slowly began to loosen reluctantly.

Mitch flipped over so that he was now lying beside her, taking great gulps of air. In a few moments his breathing had returned to normal.

"Now, let me guess. You finally got around to canning," he drawled as he reached up and picked a stray bean out of her hair.

"I think I did something wrong," she admitted in a shaky voice.

"No kidding? What makes you think that?" His blue eyes moved around the room, smothering a chuckle as he noted beans hanging from the curtains, on the TV set, and stuck all over the walls and the ceiling.

"Oh, Mitch! What have I done! Just look at this room!" she wailed.

Both sets of eyes traveled around the room this time. For a moment all was silent. Then a deep chuckle started in the bottom of Mitch's throat, erupting into outright hilarity. His large body shook, and in moments he was doubled up with laughter. Shannon tried not to follow his ludicrous example, since she viewed the situation as anything but funny! But within seconds she had joined his laughter, both of them rolling in a gigantic puddle of green beans.

"Stop that laughing," Shannon scolded, tears beginning to run freely down her face as their hilarity continued to mount. "Marla is going to kill me! That stupid pressure cooker lid went right through the kitchen screen!"

"Don't I know it!" Mitch laughed gleefully. "If I hadn't shoved Mr. Parks out of the way, it would have hit him on top of his bald head!"

They both erupted into another uncontrollable fit of laughter.

When she was finally able to get herself under control, Shannon rolled back over and faced Mitch, only to break out in a new fit of giggles when she remembered how pale his face had been when he had come bursting through the doorway.

Mitch gathered her up in his arms, still laughing. "Shannon Wranebow, you are priceless!" Shannon flinched inwardly as he called her by her married name.

"I still don't know what I did wrong! I canned the other jars without the least bit of trouble. Maybe I had the burner turned on too high," she speculated between giggles.

"I'd say that the pressure cooker had a faulty safety valve." Mitch grinned. "I don't think even *you* could get a lid to blow off like that one did unless there was a defect somewhere. Usually, only the steam cap would blow."

Shannon lifted her brown gaze up to meet his twinkling blue eyes. "You must think I have a screw loose."

"Now, did I say that?" He smiled back at her tenderly, then reached out to retrieve another stray green bean from her hair. "I may have thought it, but I sure didn't say it!"

Shannon punched him playfully, suddenly becoming aware of the position they were in. They were still lying together on the floor, locked tightly in each other's embrace. Her hands dropped from his chest shyly as she

78

became aware of her bare legs pressed against his bare ones. They were both wearing shorts, and while Shannon had a halter on, Mitch was without his shirt again. For a moment she had to fight the crazy urge to run her fingers through the thick hair that covered his broad chest. Her breathing quickened as she involuntarily drank in the familiar smell and feel of her ex-husband.

"Hey"—Mitch tipped her face up to meet his—"what would you say if I asked you to have dinner with me tonight? There's a wonderful restaurant at the lodge on the other side of the lake."

"Tonight?" Shannon avoided meeting his gaze.

"Yes, tonight. We've both been working our tails off around here, and I don't know about you, but I don't think I can face one more peanut butter sandwich today."

"I . . ." She wanted to accept his offer so badly that it was almost a physical pain, and yet, she certainly didn't want to reopen old wounds. "I don't think so. . . . It will probably take me hours to clean up this mess."

"No, it won't. Not if I help," he persisted, his fingers still touching her face, "and unless you specifically tell me to go back across that damn chalk line, I'm going to insist on helping you."

"You don't have to. You didn't make the mess," she countered uneasily. She knew she should pull out of his embrace, but it felt so good to be back in his arms again.

"We're both in this thing together," he replied matter-of-factly, rising to his feet and pulling her along beside him. "Besides, now that I've been relieved of my garden, I don't have anything to do at the moment anyway."

"I'm sorry about that little incident. . . ." Shannon mumbled apologetically.

79

"A week ago I would have kissed you for destroying it, but now I think I'm going to miss the damn thing," he admitted.

"You can have mine," she offered generously.

"Thanks, but no thanks," he returned, grinning at her.

Their eyes fastened once again on the room they were standing in. Any unsuspecting onlooker would have sworn the war of the worlds had just been fought in it with green beans as the ammunition.

Shannon heaved a deep sigh. "I don't even know where to begin," she confessed.

Mitch walked over to the sink and withdrew a pail and scrub brush from beneath the counter. Filling it with hot water and cleanser, he stepped back over and handed the pail to her. "You start with this, I'll get a mop."

Shannon frowned as she thought of the monumental chore ahead of them.

"Don't frown like that," Mitch scolded good-naturedly as he walked to the broom closet. "Personally, I just thank God you weren't canning bullets!"

CHAPTER FIVE

It took a little over two hours to mop, sweep, and clean the entire kitchen and a section of the living area. When they were finally through, they both admitted that neither one of them ever wanted to see another green bean as long as they lived.

While Mitch was finishing the last of the mopping, Shannon accepted his suggestion that she use the bathroom first. Gratefully, she showered away the remains of her horrible afternoon, letting the water spray over her tired body. If it hadn't been for Mitch's help, she would still be cleaning this time tomorrow. She smiled as she toweled herself dry and dusted with a fragrant powder. Funny, but she had forgotten how helpful he had been while they were married. Saturdays had always been a big day for her. Laundry, grocery shopping, and the interminable chores of housekeeping. She had worked at the store part time in those days, but it seemed she was always behind when Saturday rolled around. Mitch would get up when she did, and after a leisurely breakfast, he would usually offer to help her. Within a few hours they would have the apartment clean, the laundry done, and the groceries put away. For the rest of the day they would do the things they both enjoyed most. It was not unusual to find them making love in the late afternoon, then napping for a while in each other's arms.

Shannon shook her head to rid herself of those painful memories. That part of her life was over. If Mitch had loved her enough to give up his job, there never would have been a divorce, but unfortunately, his profession meant more to him than his wife did. Resentment overtook her feelings now as she slipped on a robe and left the bathroom. She had just begun to spend a few hours a day without thinking of Mitch before Marla and Jerry's accident. Now, she would have to start forcing herself to forget him all over again when she returned home.

The phone rang as she was just slipping her dress over her head. She heard Mitch answer it, then listened as he talked for a moment. In a few moments he hung up the receiver and went into the bathroom.

Shannon finished dressing, then went into the kitchen to wait for him. Minutes later he emerged from the bathroom fully dressed and cleanly shaven.

"Knock-knock."

"Come in," Shannon returned courteously.

"Are you about ready?"

"Yes. Who was on the phone earlier?" Shannon reached for her purse and walked toward the front door.

"Cliff Webster."

"Oh? What did he want?" They both stepped out into the early summer evening. Mitch took Shannon's arm and pointed her toward the boat dock. "Let's take the boat. I know the way."

"That sounds nice. What did Cliff want?" Shannon asked again as they strolled toward the lake to the sound of hundreds of jarflies tuning up.

"You."

Shannon whirled and looked at him sharply. "Me?"

"Yeah, but I told him you were busy."

"Really." Her eyes flashed dangerously. "Did it ever occur to you I might not be too *busy* to speak with him?"

"It occurred to me, but I figured he didn't want anything too important."

"How could you know that?" she asked coolly.

"Because I asked him if it was important, and he said it wasn't. I figured he's trying to put the make on you, that's all," he replied nonchalantly.

"Mitchell." Shannon paused and angrily placed her hands on her hips. "From now on you 'figure' on your own time and leave my time alone!"

"Oh, you would just love that, wouldn't you? I've told you before, Shannon, Cliff Webster is just looking for some action. You better stay away from him!"

"That's your opinion. Maybe I happen to think he's a very attractive man!" Shannon fired back. Of course, she *didn't* think he was an attractive man. On the contrary, she didn't like him, but Mitch was never going to know that!

"Yeah, you probably do think that," he agreed, a brief shaft of pain flashing across his handsome features. "He *would* be just your type."

"What do you mean by 'just my type'?"

"I mean, he's got a nice safe job in a hospital. That should put a big plus sign in his column," Mitch returned snidely. "You could eagerly look forward to him returning home to your welcoming arms every night; that is, if he didn't get hit by an ambulance on the way out of work!"

"You're being absurd! I've barely met the man, and you have us practically married!"

83

"Well, admit it! Wouldn't you just love to have a man like Cliff?" Mitch persisted hotly.

"Yes!" she practically shouted. "I *would* love to have a man with a nice safe job!"

"See?" Mitch's temper cooled immediately. "That's what I was trying to tell you," he said. "But, mark my words, Shannon, you would never be happy with a man like that."

"You're nuts!" Shannon announced, angrily walking past him toward the boat.

"I may be, but I happen to know the girl I married. She likes her men to be men. Not pantywaists."

"You no longer should be concerned about the girl you married. That's all water under the bridge," she said.

"I still have my memories," he said quietly as he trotted to catch up with her. "And, if you'll admit it, you have yours."

"I'm working very hard to rid myself of those memories. I suggest you do the same."

He smiled. "I am, but I don't seem to be having much success."

"Well, keep trying. I'm certainly going to," she said.

He shrugged his broad shoulders indifferently as he helped her into the pleasure boat. "Good luck!"

The sun was a fiery round orange ball in the western sky as Mitch and Shannon pulled away from the dock in Marla and Jerry's eighteen-foot runabout. The powerful boat cut smoothly through the water as Mitch idled slowly out of the mouth of the cove.

Without a doubt this was Shannon's favorite part of the day. The intense heat had passed as the sun settled gently over a distant hilltop casting its red glow over the lake. The waters lay tranquil as the boaters returned to their campsites or motels for the evening. Only the early evening fishermen with their impressive "bass" boats were out running at top speed down the lake, their occupants' faces radiant with the expectancy of getting the "big" one tonight!

As Mitch shoved the lever down next to the steering wheel, Shannon felt the boat surge forward, running smoothly out of the cove, heading for open waters.

A sense of exhilaration washed over her as the boat continued to pick up speed, racing quietly through the placid waters. All the cares of the day were forgotten as she leaned her head back against the seat, enjoying the feel of the wind whipping through her hair.

Mitch smiled at her as he reached down and inserted a tape into the tape casette deck.

The air was immediately filled with stereophonic music as Living Strings sweetly performed the theme from *Romeo and Juliet.* Shannon could see brightly burning campfires dotting the shoreline as campers prepared their evening meals. Happy, carefree children played along the edge of the water, throwing rocks into the lake.

All too soon the boat was gliding into the cove of Cedar Lane Lodge. Mitch pulled up alongside the pier as one of the young boys employed by the lodge gave them a helping hand. The attendant had the boat secured to the dock in a matter of minutes and was running over to offer his services to another incoming guest.

Mitch stepped out of the boat and turned to reach for Shannon. Before she was aware of his intentions, he had lifted her out of the boat and set her down on the dock next to him.

"That wasn't necessary," she said in a breathless voice.

His touch had sent shivers running down her spine for the second time that day.

"It was to me," he dismissed curtly. "How about us both forgetting the past . . . at least for this evening and enjoy a night out?"

Before she could agree, or disagree, he had taken her hand and had begun walking down the aisle of the boat dock that housed all the rental fishing and pleasure boats belonging to the lodge.

Several people were sitting on benches fishing, their red bobbers bouncing merrily in the waters as swarms of perch that lived around the dock bit playfully at their hooks. A young couple, obviously honeymooners, lay on the swimming dock, exchanging kisses, reluctant to give up the fading day.

Walking slowly up the concrete ramp that led to the restaurant, Mitch and Shannon reveled in the beauty of the peaceful summer eve. They were still unconsciously holding hands as they reached the lodge, and Mitch asked for a table for two. Minutes after the hostess had seated them at a table overlooking the lake, a waitress brought their water and menu, her blue eyes openly admiring Mitch. Casting one last appreciative glance in his direction, she left them alone to study the menu.

"What looks good to you?" he asked absently.

"Anything!" Shannon said enthusiastically. "I mean, anything *but* cold cereal."

"Or peanut butter," he added. "How about a steak?"

"Sounds good."

"Or spaghetti?"

"Sounds great!"

"Or . . . let's see, how about chicken?"

"Sounds delicious!"

86

Mitch glanced up from behind his menu. "Which one? Steak, spaghetti, or chicken?"

"All of the above. I feel like I haven't eaten in a month!" she confirmed with an enchanting grin.

If the waitress thought their order of chicken, steak, spaghetti, and three pieces of apple pie was unusual, she didn't indicate it. She was still too busy looking Mitch over, marveling at his unusual good looks.

When she finally left the table, Shannon couldn't help but take offense at her blatant perusal of her ex-husband.

"Did you see the way she looked at you?" Shannon asked irritably.

"No! Was she looking at me?" Mitch scoffed in mock horror, a wicked grin accompanying his words.

"You know darn well she was." Shannon caught her temper as Mitch's grin continued to widen.

He reached over and captured her hand back in his. "Does it matter to you how other women look at me?" he asked seriously.

"No, certainly not," she protested, quickly removing her hand from his. "I just thought she was a bit nervy, that's all."

"That's a shame." Mitch sighed. "I was hoping it would."

Shannon turned her head toward the window, fixing her gaze on the shimmering lake. Mitch unnerved her when he talked like that.

"That's not what you said the other day. You said you were glad our marriage was over," she reminded him, still stung by the hateful words they had thrown at each other the first day they arrived.

"I've said quite a lot of things to you that I regretted

87

later," he acknowledged quietly. "I'd like to think you've said things you didn't mean, either."

"I can't think of anything I've said that I didn't mean," she returned stubbornly.

"Oh? Then I guess I have to assume you've meant every word you said in the last year."

"Yes. I guess you will," she replied, trying to fight back the rising tears. She had been determined that this evening she wouldn't let the discussion turn toward their previous marital problems, but it seemed clear that it was heading in that direction.

Mitch's troubled gaze found the restful waters of the lake as they sat in an uncomfortable silence.

"You know," Mitch began reflectively a few minutes later, "I could never understand Jerry's need to buy that old resort until lately. I've been here before, but now I realize that this place could really get in your blood. Just look at that lake."

Shannon's eyes feasted on the beauty stretched out miles before her. It was truly beautiful, and she could see why Marla's letters had always been so full of love and excitement for her new home in the rugged Ozark hills.

"It is very lovely," she said softly. "I can see why Marla and Jerry are so happy here."

"They have a good marriage. I envy them," Mitch returned aloofly, his eyes still gazing out across the dark waters.

"Ya—hoo . . . Mr. and Mrs. Wranebow . . ."

Shannon and Mitch glanced up at the same time to see Mr. Parks and his wife, Thelma, making their way to their table.

"Hi, there. We didn't expect to see you two over here

tonight!" Thelma smiled. "My husband told me you had a little trouble with your canning this afternoon!"

"A little, yes." Shannon smiled back. "Mitch decided we would eat out tonight," she explained sheepishly, trying to avoid Mr. Parks's laughing eyes.

"I'd say your husband is a smart man," Mr. Parks said with a chuckle. "After the day you two have put in, you both need a little relaxation!"

After several minutes of idle chatter, the Parkses finally moved on and let Mitch and Shannon eat the meal the waitress had set before them while they had been talking.

An hour later they stepped back out into the warm summer evening, both completely stuffed from their over-indulgence.

"I feel miserable!" Shannon confessed as she tried to loosen the belt on her dress. "How could we have eaten all that food?"

"At first it was easy," Mitch defended as he loosened another notch in his belt and let out a relieved sigh. "It was those last three hot rolls that did me in."

"Let's take a walk," Shannon suggested. The night was beautiful, and she didn't want it to end yet. The food and easy conversation of the last hour had put them both in a mellow mood, and they began to stroll along the shore of the lake. For a while conversation was unnecessary as they listened contentedly to the quiet lapping of the waves against the shore. The moon had risen and lit up their pathway as they walked together silently.

Mitch took a deep breath, inhaling the fresh breeze that blew off the lake. "This is nice."

It was nice. Especially when Mitch reached out and took her hand, glancing at her briefly for approval. For a moment it was on her lips to refuse permission, but as her hand enfolded in his, her mouth refused to issue the words that would halt his aggressiveness.

Between the frogs, crickets, and jarflies, the air was alive with nature's symphony. Shannon knew that she was acting unwisely, but she felt at peace as they walked hand in hand through the moon-drenched evening. Yet, this strange, uneasy feeling that Mitch was stirring within her both puzzled and frightened her. She had thought that her love for him was dead. But, if that were so, why were her legs turning weak and her stomach churning with tiny butterflies at the mere touch of his hand?

They had walked for over half an hour when they came to a plush, grassy area in back of the lodge. Pulling her to a halt, Mitch implored, "Let's rest for a minute."

"You must be getting old," Shannon chided, but dropped down on the thick grassy turf willingly.

"I think I am," he agreed, lying down flat on his back and crossing his arms in back of his head. "Help me pick out the Big Dipper."

Shannon lay down beside him, her gaze following his into the heavens. The brilliance of the stars was almost breathtaking as they began to search out various constellations, laughing together when one of them would err shamelessly in naming a particular cluster of stars.

"You always were horrible in astronomy," Shannon teased as Mitch pointed out the evening star as the planet Mars.

"I always spent my time on more important things when I was in school," he defended with a chuckle.

"Like girls?" Shannon laughed.

"Well, I certainly didn't waste all this charm on the boys!" he teased back indignantly.

"You're horrible," Shannon noted as she stared back up into the diamond-studded sky, ignoring the sexual innuendo in his voice. "Besides, whoever told you you had any charm?"

"You have. Lots of times." He rolled over on his side and leaned his head on his hand. "Now, haven't you?"

His "haven't you" was a bit too smug, in Shannon's opinion. "I don't recall," she said.

"Well"—he reached over and tipped her face toward his—"maybe I could help you remember."

"No!" Shannon jerked away nervously.

He firmly turned her head back around to face him again.

"Yes."

Shannon swallowed hard as her brown eyes cautiously met his serious blue ones.

"Mitch . . . don't start anything foolish," she warned in a trembling voice.

"I don't plan on doing anything foolish," he replied easily. He gently ran one finger along the outline of her face. "I just don't like the idea of you saying that I've never charmed you. I happen to think I have . . . many times." His voice had grown to a low, husky timbre as his finger continued to explore the familiar contour of her silken features. "Now, are you going to tell me you don't remember that either?"

"That's right, I don't remember that either," she returned stubbornly. She was sure he heard her heart pounding.

"Tsk, tsk, tsk," he chastised. "Such a lovely little liar." Shannon stiffened as she watched his mouth move closer to hers.

"Mitch . . . don't . . ." Her words were muffled as

his mouth closed over hers. Shannon's eyes closed involuntarily as the feel of his lips on hers sent shivers racing down her spine. He kissed her slowly, lightly, and very thoroughly.

When their lips parted moments later, his breathing was soft and ragged.

"Was that charming enough, Mrs. Wranebow?" he asked softly.

"It's *Ms.* Murphy, and I didn't notice," she lied.

"Sorry, I still think of you as Mrs. Wranebow," he apologized insincerely. "And, try to pay attention this time." His mouth came back to hers slowly and seductively. Her arms came up around his neck as she lifted her face for his kiss with no longer any thought of refusing his advances. This time the kiss was longer, deeper, his tongue probing intimately with hers. Mitch had always been a master at arousing her quickly, and he was fast proving that he could still bring her to the point of being senseless with no trouble.

She heard a small whimper and was surprised to find that it had come from her, as she felt his fingers slide up her arm and slip the strap of her sundress down off her shoulder. His hand reached inside the thin material and found what it was searching for with the greatest of ease.

Gently he squeezed her breast, a low groan escaping from his throat. "Tell me you don't remember this," he demanded in a harsh whisper.

"I don't!" Shannon's senses were reeling. She should stop him. They had always had an active sex life during their marriage, and she knew that it would only be a matter of moments before they would be engaged in something they both would regret later.

"Then, how about this?" he persisted as his mouth

moved down to lazily plant kisses along the soft brown crest he held in his hand now.

That small, traitorous whimper appeared again as his mouth moved from one budding breast to the next, his tongue teasing and probing mercilessly in its attempt to bring forth a confession out of her.

What he was doing was just plain dirty pool! Shannon thought as she buried her hands in the thick mass of black curls on his head. He knew what effect he had always had on her, and it made her mad to think he was using this cheap ploy to prove his arrogant, chauvinistic point!

"Nothing familiar yet?" he queried.

"No, nothing. I think I should be going—" Shannon gasped out loud as his hand slid beneath her dress and instantly got down to serious business.

"Mitch," she protested weakly, her body springing alive under his bold, intimate caresses. He was being extremely rotten this time! "Stop that this instant!" she demanded helplessly. Actually, she would be willing to give him at least another twenty minutes, but he was acting so arrogant she wouldn't have dared.

"Did I finally ring a bell?" he asked hopefully, his mouth searing hers again with another round of fiery kisses.

Ring a bell! Mercy! Was he joking? Every fiber in her was clanging! It simply wasn't fair, she steamed as she moaned ecstatically once again. He should be made to pay for this . . . this . . . travesty!

Well, Mr. Wranebow! Two could play this game! Her hand shot out and passionately gripped the front of his shirt. "All right, darling, I give! I remember everything," she confessed in a sexy voice.

Mitch blinked, his mind in a hazy, passionate stupor. "You do?"

"Oh, you bet!" she assured in her sexiest tone. Her hand pulled violently at the top button of his shirt, sending it spiraling into the dark night. "I remember how I used to undress you"—the second button popped off—"and run my little fingers through all this delicious hair"—the third and fourth buttons joined the first and second swiftly. In the blink of an eye, Shannon had peeled Mitch's shirt back and buried her face in the warm flesh of his chest while her hands efficiently unsnapped his belt and trousers.

"Hey," Mitch groaned, his breathing labored and heavy. "Slow down a little!"

"I can't! You just turn me to oatmeal every time I'm around you," she said in a clipped, sharp tone, her hand running down the front of his trousers with the speed of light.

Mitch sucked in his breath and moaned again. "Come on, sweetheart, slow down!" he pleaded as her hands became bolder.

"Am I bringing back old memories, darling? Remember the times when we've lain in each other's arms and made love all night long?" Her hands moved seductively over his bare flesh. "And surely you haven't forgotten how you used to get soooo . . . excited when I would do this to you." Her hands worked in smooth, easy movements.

"Shannon. . . ." Mitch caught her hands and stopped them, his smoldering gaze capturing hers. "Cut it out, unless you're serious!" he demanded sternly.

"Serious? Why of course I'm serious. Aren't you?" The game had suddenly turned tasteless to both of them.

Shannon felt so sexually frustrated she could have screamed. She longed to sink back to his arms and let him take her to the passionate paradise that she knew all too well was waiting for her. But she wasn't about to jump back in his bed and have him laugh at her inability to resist his so called "charms"!

"If you mean, am I willing to make love to you, then, yes, I'm more than willing! It doesn't take a genius to see that! But, somehow, I get the strange impression you're not serious."

"Give the little man a prize!" Shannon bounded to her feet, angrily fixing her dress. "You're right! I have no intentions of crawling back in your bed! I thought I made that perfectly clear the first day we arrived!"

"Oh, you made it clear!" Mitch shouted, springing to his feet and adjusting his pants and buckling his belt angrily. "But I thought you were just being your old damn pigheaded stubborn self! You want me as bad as I want you, and don't try to deny it!"

"We are divorced, Mitch! Can't you get that through your thick head?"

"Our divorce was a mistake!" he shouted. "For once, why don't you admit the truth? If you had listened to reason, we would still be married today!"

"You cared more about your job than you did your wife. . . ."

"Don't give me that garbage! I loved you, and you knew it."

"Then why did you let the divorce go through uncontested?" she demanded hotly. This was the first time she had mentioned how she felt about him not contesting the divorce. She had always been upset about how he had so coldly let the final papers go through, and just thinking about it still hurt her deeply.

Mitch glared at her defiantly, then heaved an exasperated sigh, burying his hands in his unruly dark curls. "Dammit, I never thought you were really serious about getting the divorce, Shannon! I thought you were bluffing, and I figured I'd simply wait until you came to your senses and grew up," he confessed. "By the time the final papers were served, I was so shocked to find out you were serious, I blew up. If you were that hell-bent on getting a divorce, then I wasn't about to stand in your way."

Shannon felt nearly sick with remorse to think that her marriage could possibly have been saved with simple communication. "I'm sorry, Mitch," she said quietly. "I thought you knew I don't make idle threats."

"I do now," he said.

"Well, that's all in the past," Shannon reminded him tearfully. "We would probably never have seen each other again if it hadn't been for this accident . . ."

"You're right. I suppose it would be too much to hope for . . . a reconciliation?" His serious blue eyes met hers hopefully.

"You still have your job," she pointed out.

"And, apparently, you haven't grown up yet!" he returned sharply.

"Apparently, I haven't!" she shot back crossly.

"You still want the world on a nice safe platter, don't you?"

"Not the world, just my husband."

"Well, then I might just have to see what I can do to help you realize your dream, Ms. Murphy." Mitch smiled at Shannon wickedly, pulling his opened shirt together and stuffing it into his pants.

"Just what do you mean by that?" she asked suspiciously as they started the long walk back around the lake to their boat. "I don't need your help to find a husband!"

"Oh, but you do, sweetheart! With me to point out all your lovely assets, we'll snag you a nice safe husband in no time at all!" He put his arm around her waist cockily. "And I have just the creep—man in mind," he amended quickly.

"You're nuts!"

"No, I don't think so. You'll see. It will all work out perfectly!"

"Would you care to clue me in on who the lucky man is going to be?"

"Why, of course not, darling. He's already hanging around, panting on your doorstep, just ripe for the pluckin'," he assured her in a confident voice.

Shannon stopped and put her hands on her hips. "Who's right for the 'pluckin'?"

Mitch smiled, then leaned down and gave her a friendly kiss on her nose. "Why, Cliff Webster, sweetheart. Who else?"

CHAPTER SIX

Shannon was still steaming by the time they reached home. The very audacity of that . . . that . . . ant-brain! Trying to pawn her off on Cliff Webster, of all people!

She had been so shocked by Mitch's ludicrous statement that she had stared at him with her mouth gaping open. Then the full implication had assaulted her, and her temper had exploded. She hadn't spoken one word to him on the way home and had slammed the door in his face as they both entered the house.

By morning her temper had stilled, but not subsided.

"Knock-knock!"

Shannon stonily refused to answer her imaginary door as she sat calmly stirring her coffee at the kitchen table.

"Come on, damn it, I know you heard me," Mitch chided her irritably.

There was nothing but silence from Shannon's side of the chalk line. When they had cleaned up yesterday after the explosion, they had erased the line, but she had redrawn it this morning.

"I'm going to the hospital this morning. Are you coming with me or not?" he asked.

Shannon picked up the cream pitcher and poured some

in her coffee, then leafed casually through the morning paper.

"Okay. At least you can't accuse me of not asking," he replied calmly. "I thought we'd stop somewhere on the way and have a nice big breakfast; bacon and eggs, hot biscuits, hash browns . . ."

Shannon's stomach rumbled. As of yet she hadn't been able to face the box of cold cereal this morning.

". . . peach jam, hot coffee, orange juice . . ." he continued temptingly.

"I'll be ready in five minutes," she relented, tossing the paper aside and scurrying into the bathroom.

After the promised breakfast, she felt in much better spirits as they drove to the hospital together. The day was hazy and hot, and Shannon welcomed the cool air conditioning of Mitch's Mercedes.

The hospital was bustling this morning as they rode up on the elevator to Marla and Jerry's floor.

They were in a private room now, and it closely resembled a greenhouse, with tables of plants and flowers crowding the small quarters.

Mitch had to duck to keep from hitting his head on a giant fern hanging on Jerry's traction bar.

"How do you put up with all this?" Mitch asked with a grimace as he brushed fern leaves off his shoulders.

"I'm getting used to it." Jerry sighed with resigned patience. "Marla won't let the nurses take any of these flowers out. She loves all of them."

"Of course I love all of them," Marla said brightly. "I can't believe everyone has been so marvelous! Look at this, Shannon. It arrived a few minutes ago." She held up a large yellow plant for her sister's perusal.

While the girls chatted happily, Mitch pulled up a chair and sat down next to Jerry's bed. "How's it going?"

"Slow," Jerry replied glumly. "I'm afraid I make a very poor patient."

Mitch laughed. "I know I would!"

"How are things going at home?" Jerry asked worriedly.

"Shannon and I are handling things," Mitch assured him. "The business is still intact."

"Man, I'll be so glad to get out of here. . . ." Jerry's voice trailed off painfully as he leaned back against his pillow and closed his eyes.

"Darling? Are you all right?" Marla glanced over at her husband anxiously.

"I'm fine, Marla," he answered listlessly.

"You're looking much better," Shannon assured as she walked over and stood before him. "A few more weeks and you'll be back home as good as new." She laughed. "And, believe me, I'm going to be more than happy to turn it all back over to you!"

Jerry smiled and reached for her hand. "What's the matter? Aren't you enjoying your vacation?"

"I can't think of anywhere I'd rather be." She grinned coyly.

"Does she look sincere to you?" Jerry looked at Mitch skeptically.

"She doesn't say things she doesn't mean," Mitch confirmed with an indifferent shrug.

Shannon glanced over at her ex-husband, their eyes meeting briefly.

"Mitch is right. I don't say things I don't mean. And I'm more than happy to be able to help you and Marla out when you need me. After all, we're all family, aren't we?"

"Yes, but I don't know how we'll ever be able to repay you and Mitch," Marla broke in. "I shudder to think what would have happened to the resort if you two hadn't taken over."

"It would have all worked out," Shannon argued. "Now, I'll help you into the bathroom, and let's see if we can do something about your hair."

"It's a hideous mess!" Marla agreed readily.

It took a few minutes for Marla to negotiate herself out of bed, even with Shannon's help. Then they disappeared into the small bathroom.

"How are things really going?" Jerry persisted as the door to the bathroom closed.

"I told you, everything's fine," Mitch assured him again.

"I'm not talking about the resort. I'm talking about you and Shannon," Jerry said.

"Oh. Well"—Mitch laughed ironically—"what can I tell you? I don't happen to be one of Shannon's favorite people right now."

"You two still slugging it out?"

"No. Basically we get along all right. As long as she stays on her side of the room, and I stay on mine."

Jerry looked at Mitch in a questioning manner.

Mitch shrugged his shoulders. "She's got some damn chalk line drawn down the center of the house."

Jerry grinned. "And you let her?"

"Hell, I can't control her! I found that out a long time ago."

"You're still in love with her, so why don't you take

her over your knee and show her who's boss?" Jerry suggested, his grin growing broader.

"I value my life more than that," Mitch replied gruffly.

"You realize, I didn't hear you deny that you were still in love with her," Jerry pursued.

Mitch got up out of his chair and walked over to the window, his hands shoved deeply into the pockets of his trousers. He stared out on the street a few minutes, collecting his thoughts before he spoke. "No, I can't say that I'm not still in love with her."

"So, why don't you go for it? What better opportunity to win her back than the position you've been forced into?"

"She hates me. She thinks my job meant more to me than our marriage." Mitch's face clouded with unwanted memories. "That's not true, Jerry. I loved her more than any one thing in the world. But when Dad died, I felt obligated to finish the building for him. You know how much it meant to him, and I was the only one that could do it."

"I don't think he would have wanted it finished at the expense of your marriage," Jerry pointed out reluctantly. "After all, I was raised in the steel business too, but I sure didn't feel any obligation to finish the job. I promised Marla I would never risk my life like that again. That's the main reason we bought the resort. Hell, Mitch, I was always thinking about an accident nearly every time I went up. I'm more than glad to be down on solid ground, and if you weren't so stubborn, you'd admit you're not crazy about the dangers you face every day yourself."

"I didn't say I don't think about them. I do. Every time I'm standing up there five hundred and fifty feet in the air! As soon as this building is finished, I'll climb down and never go back up."

"What happens if you never climb back down?" Jerry asked solemnly. "Look what happened to Dad?"

Mitch turned to face his brother, his features mirroring defeat. "Now you sound just like her!"

"She has a point, Mitch. Why not leave the rest of the job to the fellows that still love the thrill and exhilaration of their work? We've been in it too long. It's time to let the other guy take the risks."

"What difference does it make now? My marriage is over, and Shannon sure isn't in any mood for reconciliation," Mitch conceded grimly.

"Then find yourself someone new. You're a man meant for marriage and a permanent relationship with one woman." Jerry grinned again. "Unless you've changed in the last few months. I know there're a lot of willing women out there."

"Yeah, there sure are. And one of them happens to be staying at your place of business. The redhead in cottage nine. She is driving me nuts! If she didn't think Shannon and I were married, I would have been raped days ago!"

"Raped? Now come on, Mitch. I remember her. You're surely not *that* soured on women."

A disconcerted grin crossed Mitch's handsome features. "Well, maybe not raped. But I don't like for a woman to come on so strong. At least, not just any woman."

"You wouldn't have any objections to your ex-wife being a little pushy though, would you?"

Mitch's mind skipped back to Shannon's outrageous seduction of him the night before. "None at all."

"Why don't you use the redhead to make Shannon

jealous? Maybe a little competition will open her eyes and make her see what she's missing," Jerry suggested wickedly.

"I've thought of that, but I decided that I couldn't stand the punishment myself!" Mitch admitted. "Rhonda is more woman than I want to tackle."

"Say." Jerry pulled himself up in bed, his mind plotting feverishly. "Have you tried the 'sweep her off her feet' approach?"

"I tried it already. She 'swept' me right back into a defeated heap!" It still smarted every time he thought about the night before and Shannon's rejection of his "charms."

"Why don't you just go out and buy a new car or something and forget about women for the time being?" Jerry offered helpfully.

"Somehow, the thought of sleeping with a car isn't half as tempting as sleeping with a beautiful, sexy woman. I do believe your brains have been affected by this accident," Mitch said dryly.

"Only trying to help!" Jerry grinned affectionately.

"Well, don't. I can take care of my personal life without any help from family," Mitch cautioned. "Besides, I have a plan."

"Oh?"

The door to the bathroom opened, and Shannon and Marla returned to the room.

"Do I look any better?" Marla preened before the two brothers.

"Any better than what?" Jerry asked innocently.

"Any better than I did ten minutes ago," Marla said indignantly.

"I can't remember what you looked like ten minutes ago," Jerry deadpanned. "Do you, Mitch?"

"No. I don't even remember the cute chick she's got with her." He gave Shannon a sexy wink.

Marla shook her head hopelessly as she hobbled over to the side of her husband's bed and wrapped her arms around his neck carefully. "Kiss me, you big lug."

Both Mitch and Shannon had to turn away from the couple who were exchanging a long, delicious kiss. A look of pain was evident on both their faces as they discreetly kept their eyes averted from each other. At one time, not so very long ago, they would have been doing the same crazy, loving thing.

Mitch cleared his throat and stood up abruptly. "If you two think you can break it up, Shannon and I better be going."

Marla and Jerry broke apart embarrassedly. "We're sorry. . . ."

"Don't worry about it." Shannon leaned over and hugged Marla. "Just thank God you have someone who loves you like Jerry does," she whispered in her sister's ear.

"Thanks for coming today." Marla returned the hug with affection. "And, don't worry, things will get better." She smiled at Shannon encouragingly.

Mitch and Shannon said their good-byes and left the hospital shortly before noon. The ride home was silent. Being in the presence of happily married couples was still a strain that neither one felt up to this morning. The unpleasant altercation of the night before had put them both in a surly, irritable mood.

"You didn't finish that patch of mowing by cottage

nine!" Shannon told him crossly as the car pulled into the resort. "You said you'd finish the mowing."

"When have I had time?" Mitch shot back. He wasn't about to tell her Rhonda had been lounging around on her porch, lying in wait for him.

"You have more time than I do!" Shannon grumbled.

"That's a laugh."

"Are you implying I don't do my part?"

"Hell, no, I wasn't implying anything! I merely stated I haven't had time to finish the mowing!"

The car slid to an impatient halt as Mitch turned off the ignition and got out of his side of the car.

"You have no right to be so cranky!" Shannon complained as she slammed out of her side of the car. They both strode angrily up to the porch of the house, hot and out of sorts with the world, reaching for the door handle at the same time.

"You first!" Mitch snapped curtly.

"I wouldn't dream of it. You first!" Shannon motioned haughtily toward the door with one hand.

"Stubborn," Mitch grumbled under his breath.

Shannon glared at him defiantly. "Did you say something?" she gritted between clenched teeth.

"Nope." Mitch shoved past her and stepped into the doorway, nearly knocking her off the steps.

"You big bully!" she retaliated, jerking the screen open angrily. "The happiest day of my life was when our divorce was final!"

"Yeah, that was nice, wasn't it? I remember I sat and laughed all day," Mitch responded dryly, unperturbed by her temper tantrum.

"Oh, Mitchelllll. . . ." A sexy voice called from the distance.

106

Mitch's eyes shot up, and he swore heatedly under his breath. "Now you've done it! I bet she heard every word we said!"

Shannon glanced back over her shoulder and saw Rhonda making her way toward them, clad in skimpy shorts and a halter top that didn't quite cover all her ample assets.

"Gee, look who's coming. Little Miss Muffet," Shannon hissed sarcastically. "No doubt, she's wanting you to come over and sit on her tuffet!"

"No doubt! And your big mouth has now made it abundantly clear I'm free to come over and sit on the damn thing!"

"If you can't handle your women, I'm sure I can't help you," she said with a saccharine grin.

Mitch grunted as she slid past him and poked him in the stomach playfully.

"Hi, Rhonda!" she heard Mitch say with false enthusiasm as she walked into the kitchen. She was still grinning as she imagined Mitch trying to get free from the redhead's clutches. Serves him right! she thought spitefully as she went inside to change her clothes. Still, she kept a close watch from her bedroom window until she saw Rhonda returning to her cottage, alone, twenty minutes later.

It was nearing dark when she and Mitch went to their "corners" for dinner. He had finished the mowing that afternoon, along with several minor repairs, and she had worked in the garden. They had both stayed busy until they could no longer see to complete their tasks.

"Knock-knock!"

Shannon looked up disinterestedly from her bowl of cereal. "What is it?"

"I'll make you a deal."

Shannon eyed him suspiciously. "What kind of a deal?"

"I'll trade you two . . . now mind you, I said *two* . . . nice plump, fresh"—he rattled a bread sack in the air—"peanut butter *and* jelly sandwiches for just one bowl of your 'Munchy Crunchy Yumm Yumm' cereal."

Shannon looked longingly at the sack of bread and jar of peanut butter sitting on the floor beside Mitch's chair. After her almost steady diet of cold cereal, it looked like a top sirloin to her.

"Only one bowl?"

"Just one," Mitch bargained.

Shannon glanced back down at the tasteless bowl of cereal before her.

"Okay," she relented. Rising to her feet, she walked over to the cabinet and withdrew a small cereal bowl.

"Oh, now, come on. Be fair. I'm giving you two sandwiches," he pleaded as he surveyed the small bowl. "The least you can do is let me choose the bowl."

"You would cheat."

"No, I wouldn't," he promised solemnly.

Shannon heaved a long sigh. "All right, but you have to promise to spread the peanut butter and jelly on thick."

"I promise," he agreed angelically. "Can I come in now and get my bowl?"

"I suppose."

Five minutes later Mitch pretended to open a door, then swaggered in the room casually, kicking the pretended door shut dramatically with the back of his heel. "Good evening, Ms. Murphy. Nice weather we've been

108

having, isn't it?" He handed her the two promised sandwiches.

"Just get the cereal bowl and go back to your cage," she said, trying to ignore him.

Mitch walked over to the cabinets and started rummaging through the dishes, looking for his bowl. Minutes later he extracted a large casserole dish and handed it to her. "Here, this looks big enough."

Shannon stared at the bowl in his hand. "You're sure? There's an old tin tub at the back of the house that might hold a little bit more than this," she said snidely.

"Nope, this will do fine."

"If I wasn't so sick of this box of cereal, I would fight you on this, but actually, you're going to be doing me a favor," she told him smugly as she dumped out the cereal into his bowl. "The sooner it's gone, the sooner I can change flavors."

"Just don't get anything with peanut butter in it," he said, his eyes greedily watching the plump, tasty flakes spill out into the bowl.

"Here." She shoved the bowl into his hands.

"Looks delicious," he said. "Where's the milk?"

"Nothing was said about milk," Shannon reminded him curtly as she eagerly bit into her sandwich.

"I don't get any milk?"

"The 'deal' was, one bowl of cold cereal for two peanut butter and jelly sandwiches. Period."

"Well, hell . . ."

"Don't 'well, hell' me! You were the one who made the offer," she mumbled heartlessly while her tongue tried to dislodge a gob of peanut butter from the roof of her mouth.

Hours later Shannon was sorry she hadn't let him have

the stupid milk. The sound of dry crunching noises filled the cottage long into the hot night, grating on Shannon's nerves unmercifully.

The days dragged on. Days of hard work, long hours, and ever-growing tension between the estranged couple. It was beginning to be a living hell for Shannon. She had known that it would be hard to live in the same house with Mitch. She flinched as she recalled how they had nearly come to blows over what brand of pickles they should buy while they were finally stocking their food supply. At the time she had agreed to this living arrangement, she had thought what she had once felt for him had safely passed. Now, she wasn't so sure. As each day drew to a close, she grew into the habit of going down to the banks of the lake to watch the orange ball of sun sink behind the rugged Ozark mountains. As she would sit staring out across the peaceful waters, the terrible reality of what she feared most began to eat away at her inner self. She still loved Mitchell Wranebow. It was a frightening, soul-searing realization. She had tried so hard to put him out of her heart, and her life, and for a while she had prided herself on being successful.

Her life was a nice one now. She had a promising career, a beautiful apartment of her own, a nice car, good friends. . . . There were even one or two men she had become quite fond of. When she lay down to sleep at night, she did so with the certainty that tomorrow her day would be nearly the same as today. No worries that the man she had slept with, made love with, centered her whole world around, wouldn't return to be in her arms again the next night. Now, she *knew* that he wouldn't be there. So why, after all this time, did her heart still race and her knees grow weak and shaky when her ex-husband walked into the room and smiled at her? She would sit for hours, looking out across the wide expanse of water, wondering if she hated herself or Mitch more for causing all these old feelings of love and longing to begin to slowly crawl out of the deep, dark cavern she had so carefully buried them in months ago.

The sound of children's laughter caught her attention tonight as she sat tossing pebbles into the rippling water. Mitch was playing with the six-year-old twins who lived down the road. Huntley and Holly Daniels had taken an instant liking to Mitch and spent as much time as their mother would allow in the evening playing with their new "grown-up" friend.

Surprisingly, Mitch had been more than willing to attend the cookout at Cathy and Trevor's house, where he had met Brenda and Nathan Daniels, the twins' parents, and had even suggested that they have them over to visit some evening.

Shannon smiled to herself as another peal of infectious laughter erupted from Holly. Mitch constantly surprised Shannon on how well he got along with the children. He had never paid too much attention to children during their short marriage. Of course, Shannon knew that he wasn't ready for the responsibility of being a parent in those days. But now, he seemed to thoroughly enjoy playing with the twins in the early summer evenings. They had been playing around the lawn chair he was sprawled out in as she had walked to the water this evening, trying to bury him in the grass they had gathered from the newly mowed lawn.

Shannon had to admit that Mitch deserved a little relaxation tonight. He had spent the whole day unsucessfully trying to avoid Rhonda Neilson. That woman was driving them both up the wall with her flagrant pursuit of Mitch. Ever since Rhonda had overheard the heated spat Mitch and Shannon had had a few days ago about their divorce, she had thrown all reason to the wind and had set out to nab the eligible, good-looking Mitchell Wranebow.

Shannon had watched Rhonda's sickening performance with a tight knot in the pit of her stomach. If it hadn't been for Mitch's obvious dislike of the woman, Shannon would have cheerfully strangled her!

Shannon glanced up as Holly came running down the hill calling her name. Holding out her arms, Shannon caught her tumbling body with a breathless laugh. "Whoa, there!"

"Hi, Swannon!" Holly had a slight lisp that Shannon always found delightful.

"Hi, Holly! How are you today?"

"I'm fwine. Huntwey's been out of contwol again, as usual," she added with a resigned sigh.

"Really? Now, what has that little brother of yours been doing today?" Shannon asked sympathetically.

"Wellll . . ." Holly's brown eyes turned thoughtful. "He painted his turtle with Mommy's best fingernail polish this morning," she pointed out sternly.

"Oh, my. That is bad," Shannon agreed understandingly.

"And he cut my hair 'cause he didn't wike it wong!" she said indignantly.

"He didn't like it long?" Shannon looked at the ragged patch of hair in back of Holly's brown curls, biting her lip to keep from laughing.

"No. He wanted it showt." She nodded miserably. "Now I can't have puppy tails anymore."

Shannon hugged her close, remembering the two little ponytails Holly used to have on either side of her head. "Well, it won't be long before your hair will grow back and you'll have your puppy tails again."

Holly heaved a long, put-upon sigh. "That's what Mommy says."

Shannon laughed and hugged her again. "Mommy's right."

They both turned as Mitch let out a shrill whistle, motioning for them to join him and Huntley.

Shannon and Holly walked up the embankment holding hands and chatting together. When they reached the large tree Mitch and Huntley were sitting under, Shannon left them for a minute as she went into the house for glasses of cold lemonade and some cookies she had bought at the store that afternoon.

"This is sure good, isn't it, Mitch?" Huntley complimented, stuffing his mouth with cookies.

"It sure is," Mitch agreed, trying to avoid the spray of crumbs spewing out of the child's mouth.

Shannon glanced at Mitch and grinned as she handed Huntley a napkin. "Let's not talk with our mouth full," she cautioned gently.

"Huntwey! Mommy told you that!" Holly said in a bossy manner.

Huntley reached over to pinch his sister, knocking Mitch's glass of lemonade, sitting on the arm of his chair, into his lap.

Mitch sprang to his feet, sucking in his breath as the cold liquid seeped through the front of his trousers.

"Wow! Did you spill your lemonade, Mitch?" Huntley asked innocently.

"Yeah, sure looks like I did." Mitch mopped at his drenched trousers, ignoring Shannon's giggles.

Huntley scooted around in back of Mitch's chair and picked up his glass. Walking up to Mitch, he extended the glass graciously. "Here. You can drink some of mine."

Mitch peered into the glass Huntley extended, his stomach churning as he surveyed the soggy chunks of cookies floating in the yellow liquid.

"Hey, thanks a lot, fella, but I think I've had enough," he refused politely. "I think I'll go change my pants now," Mitch told the small group as he stepped back from the puddle of spilled lemonade. Suddenly his legs became entangled in Huntley, who had come around the back of Mitch's chair once more to pick up his discarded cookies.

For several moments Mitch fought to retain his balance and keep from falling on the twin. He staggered, groped, and flailed the air wildly before he finally fell onto the ground, tumbling head over heels down the steep embankment. When he finally reached the bottom, he sat up dazedly and looked around.

It had all happened so fast that Shannon had been unable to help him keep his balance. The three stunned faces that appeared to stare at him were indeed a funny sight.

"Did you fall down, Mitch?" Huntley asked in deep concern, completely unaware that he had been the culprit.

Shannon bit her lip, laughter welling up in her throat. She knew it wasn't funny; Mitch could have been seriously hurt, but giggles threatened to overtake her anyway.

Holly's laughter broke the silence as she burst out in giggles. "Mitch is funny!" she shrieked, thinking that he was back to entertaining them again.

"Yeah, he's a real clown!" Shannon burst out laughing. "Hey, Bozo! Are you hurt?" she called pleasantly.

"Not on your life!" he yelled back, laughter evident in his voice now. "I didn't hurt a thing!"

"I always told you you were going to break your neck one of these days," she shouted good-naturedly.

"And, I always told you, you worry too much!" he returned smugly, jumping to his feet and scrambling back up the hill. When he reached her and the twins, he grinned and tipped her face up to kiss her soundly on the tip of her nose. "You always did worry too much!" he scolded again lovingly. Their eyes met for one split second, a silent message conveyed between them.

"I know," she replied softly, "I've always been bad about that."

"Well"—his blue eyes grew serious—"we'll just have to work on changing that, won't we?"

Her eyes gazed back at him longingly. "If you'll help me."

A beautiful smile broke across his handsome features. "I'll help you," he promised.

He reached out for her hand, and she accepted willingly. "I'll go get out of these wet clothes, then we'll walk the twins home," he said happily.

They walked toward the house with a twin on each side of them, still holding each other's hands.

CHAPTER SEVEN

Whatever harmony had existed the night before, it was gone the following morning. After a night of tossing and turning, Shannon had come to some hard, cold conclusions. Mitch might talk and act as if he wanted reconciliation at times, but the fact remained, when Marla and Jerry returned from the hospital, he would be going back to St. Louis to finish the job that had torn them apart in the first place. And she would be returning to her own job, leaving the differences between them unreconciled. Those thoughts had kept her awake all night.

"Knock-knock."

"Come in," she murmured sleepily from her seat at the table.

Mitch opened the imaginary door and walked in. Without speaking, he went to the cabinet and withdrew a coffee cup and filled it from the pot on the stove.

"I want a decent breakfast this morning. What have we got?" he grumbled.

"There's eggs and bacon, but don't expect me to fix them for you," she grumbled back.

"Did I ask you to?"

"No. I was merely stating a fact."

"Well, the 'fact' is, if you won't cook, then I'll fix my own," he said irritably.

Shannon gestured toward the stove. "Be my guest."

Mitch shot her an angry glance, then rose from the table abruptly.

She sat drinking her coffee as he rattled around the kitchen, frying bacon in a loud, overbearing manner. From the corner of her eye she watched him drag down a large bowl and dump flour, shortening, salt, baking powder, and buttermilk into it. Minutes later he had fixed a pan of scrumptious-looking biscuits and popped them into a hot oven.

"Are those biscuits?" she asked hopefully, trying to keep from drooling all over herself.

"Yes. And forget it. You're not getting any," he stated bluntly.

"Who said I wanted any?" she returned indifferently.

"No one. I was merely stating a 'fact,'" he pointed out.

Out came the butter, jam, honey, and eggs from the refrigerator. He set everything but the eggs in front of her, purposely keeping the food well out of her reach.

Shannon fought unsuccessfully to block out the smell of coffee and bacon sizzling in the skillet. In another few minutes, the mouth-watering aroma of biscuits baking joined with the other smells as Shannon got out the bread to make some toast. He thought he was so darn smart! Shannon seethed miserably as she dropped the bread into the toaster and poured herself another cup of coffee. She wouldn't ask him for one of those biscuits if her life depended on it! She was positive they would be as hard as a brick, since she had never known him to be able to boil water, let alone turn out a pan of delectable, tasty, mind-boggling biscuits!

Swallowing hard, she buttered her toast and nearly

117

choked on the first bite as he reached into the oven and pulled out a pan of perfectly browned biscuits and threw them on a trivet sitting next to her coffee cup. Shannon's eyes grew fixed as she ate her unappetizing breakfast while staring at the steaming pan of flaky biscuits. Those were absolutely the best-looking pan of biscuits she had ever seen in her life!

"When did you learn to make biscuits?" she finally blurted out curiously.

Mitch dumped three fried eggs out on his plate, along with a mound of crisp bacon. "Today's the first time I ever tried it," he admitted, reaching for the butter. "I looked through the cookbook last night, and they sounded easy." He broke a biscuit apart and spread it lavishly with butter, rolling his eyes ecstatically as he bit into the hot bread. "Gad, I'm a genius!" he announced proudly.

Shannon watched silently as he sat there and devoured the huge plate of bacon and eggs along with the entire pan of hot biscuits without ever once offering her so much as a crumb!

As he was pouring his third cup of coffee, he finally remembered his manners and glanced over at her. "Your toast good this morning?" he asked pleasantly.

"Simply luscious." She smiled insincerely back at him.

He reached for the bread. "Hummmm . . . I see you've switched from white bread to the high-fiber whole wheat bread," he commented conversationally as he laid the package back down on the table and sipped his coffee in amusement.

Shannon felt her face growing warm. High fiber! She could just imagine what he was thinking now! She happened to like whole wheat with fiber whether she needed it or not!

Fortunately for Mitch, he let the subject drop.

"Let's have a cookout tonight," he said moments later.

"You don't need to worry about *my* meals," Shannon said sharply, thinking that he had finally gotten around to feeling sorry for her.

"I'm not worried about your meals," he said indifferently, "I meant, let's each ask someone over for dinner tonight."

Shannon looked at him distrustfully. "I suppose you want me to ask Cliff Webster." Mitch had been throwing them together every time Cliff wandered over to visit, which was happening almost every night now. Shannon grew irritated every time she thought about Mitch's suggestion that Cliff would make a nice *safe* husband for her.

"Say, that's a great idea! I'm glad you thought of it. Cliff would jump at the chance to spend a social evening with you," Mitch said enthusiastically.

"All right, I will, but I insist you ask Rhonda as your date," Shannon agreed smoothly, determined not to fall prey to his goading this time.

Mitch cleared his throat and moved around nervously in his chair. "Uh . . . I've been meaning to talk to you about her."

"What about her? She's still hot on your trail, isn't she?" Shannon asked.

"You might say that," Mitch agreed with a painful grimace.

"Poor baby," Shannon said sarcastically. "It must be tough having that big, bad, aggressive woman hovering over you all the time."

"That's right, it is!" Mitch said defensively.

"Now I suppose you're going to try and tell me you think she's unattractive?"

"No, she's not unattractive," he admitted. "I just happen to like to do the chasing myself."

Shannon's smile was without humor. "Naturally."

"So," he went on, ignoring her angry scowl, "I thought we might have a little cookout tonight. I figure the least you can do is help me get that Neilson character off my back while we're here."

Shannon glared at him. "The least I can do? What have *you* done that I need to repay?"

"What have I done!" he asked incredulously. "I'll tell you what I've done! I have never once failed to impress upon Cliff what a marvelous little wife you would make someone! Oh, I admit my conscience has bothered me on occasion and I've been forced to point out some of your minor flaws"—he paused and sneaked a glance in her direction to see if she was listening—"but, I only mentioned your small faults, and I must say he took them pretty well. After all, I didn't want to make you sound as if you were a saint!"

Shannon literally sizzled as she faced him. "I could break your neck, Mitchell Wranebow!"

"Of course, that's one of the first faults I had to point out," he cut in, "your nasty little temper."

She couldn't tell if he was teasing or not, but at that particular moment, it didn't matter. He had her "nasty little temper" thoroughly aroused.

"Now, Shannon, what I think we should do tonight is have you point out some of my little imperfections, if you can think of any, to Rhonda. But don't worry"—he dismissed with a wave of his hand—"I'll help you. Surely between the two of us we can come up with something."

"Surely we can!" Shannon mocked in a singsong voice. "Listen, mister, it wouldn't take me but a few minutes to give her an earful."

"Good! That's the spirit. That's all I want you to do," he said reasonably. "Lay it on thick! Lie if you have to, but just get her off my case!"

"You are absolutely crazy! I'm not going to get that woman out of your hair! Do it yourself!"

"Aw, come on, sweetheart," he pleaded innocently. "I'll help *you* get Cliff."

He looked so sincere, yet Shannon knew he was trying to goad her into saying she couldn't stand Cliff Webster. Mitch had always been the jealous type and somehow she didn't think he had changed that much, unless he really didn't care a whit about her any longer! That thought not only hurt, it made her that much madder.

"Oh, would you, darling? If I could attract a man like Cliff, I'd be the happiest woman on earth!" she gushed.

Mitch eyed her distastefully. "You would?"

"I would."

"Then you'll do it?" he asked skeptically.

"I think it's a marvelous idea. I'll call Cliff at the hospital right now." Shannon slid off her chair and rushed over to the phone. "Why don't you run right over and ask Ms. Flaming Tresses if she's available for the evening?"

"Ha! That woman's always available." Mitch slithered out of his chair and jammed his hands into his pocket. "All right, but promise me you won't screw this up, Shannon. This is the last time I want to have to worry about that pushy woman."

"I'm just like the U.S. cavalry, sweetie! You can count on me!" she told him confidently as she dialed the phone.

"But since you're obviously the master at cooking, you will be in charge of the meal."

Mitch looked momentarily disconcerted, then rallied quickly. "Okay, I can handle that!"

Shannon shook her head disgustedly as she listened to the phone ring at the other end. One pan of decent biscuits, and he thought he was Betty Crocker!

"Sure, I can handle that," Mitch repeated, still trying to convince himself that he could. "I saw a great recipe for pheasant under glass in the cookbook last night."

"Pheasant under glass! Really, Mitch! You better stick to hamburger under a bun and be satisfied," Shannon scoffed.

"We'll see," Mitch dismissed absently as he walked out of the room, scribbling down a grocery list on the back of a paper towel.

Shannon was still furious about Mitch's plans as she dressed later that evening. Cliff had indeed jumped at the opportunity to have dinner with her. Shannon had to constantly scold herself for her indifferent feelings concerning Cliff as she blew her hair dry and applied makeup. Cliff Webster was a nice guy, he just wasn't her type. And the thought of spending the whole evening watching Rhonda Neilson make a play for Mitch was tearing her apart. If Mitch hadn't made her so mad, she would have never consented to such a ridiculous suggestion, but at the time, she would have agreed to almost anything to show him how little she cared. Ha! That was a laugh. She cared all right. Too darn much for her own good!

When she was through dressing, she wandered out to

the kitchen where Mitch was busy with preparations for the forthcoming meal.

"Hi. Need any help?" she offered hesitantly.

Mitch glanced up from the cookbook and frowned. "Would you mind setting the table? I haven't had time to yet."

"Of course not," she agreed. "Are we eating in here, or outside?"

"Outside."

"That's nice." She walked over to the china hutch where Marla kept her best dishes.

"Just use paper plates," Mitch called as she withdrew four services.

"Paper plates? For pheasant under glass?" She turned and looked at him disbelievingly.

Mitch shrugged his broad shoulders. "The grocer was all out of pheasant. We're having hamburgers."

"What a shame." Shannon grinned. "I was looking forward to your amazing culinary skills."

"You'll still see them," he promised. "These hamburgers are not going to be just ordinary ones." He scooped up a gob of red meat and stared at it for a moment. "What in the hell do you do to this stuff to get it to lie flat?"

Shannon walked over and washed her hands, then took the blob of meat out of his hand. Tearing off a sheet of waxed paper, she laid the meat on it and dramatically smashed it into a ragged patty with the palm of her hand.

"Just like that," she told him smugly.

Mitch stared at the meat sickly. "That's the most disgusting-looking patty I've ever seen."

"You said you wanted a hamburger patty, not a work of art," she reminded him tightly.

"Well, can't you make them a little neater?"

"I could, if I wanted to," she replied haughtily.

"Then do it, Bright Eyes! I don't want the meat hanging over the bun when we have company," he pleaded with sincere concern.

The way he had automatically called her Bright Eyes again tore at her heartstrings. "Oh, all right! Good grief! You would think we were entertaining Emily Post," she relented. Picking up the smashed meat, she began to reshape it into a neat, rounded patty. "There! Does that meet with your approval?"

Mitch studied the shape of the patty thoughtfully. "Make it just a little fatter."

Shannon glared at him. "I'll make it a little fatter, you —" Her words were cut off as his mouth swooped down and captured hers.

For a moment she was totally stunned by his unexpected actions, but not for long. The ball of hamburger meat she had been holding fell limply back down on the table as her arms crept up around his neck, and she moved closer into his embrace. His lips moved persuasively over hers, his tongue plying hers seductively. The clean smell of his soap and after-shave assaulted her nostrils as she willingly let him deepen the kiss. His hand ran suggestively down the back of her dress, stopping at her bottom to draw her closer between his taut thighs.

A feeling of longing overcame her as he pressed her against the proof of his steadily mounting desire for her. The kiss was long and sultry, and with very little encouragement, it could grow quickly out of hand.

When his hand came up to familiarly cup her swelling breast, her senses returned momentarily.

"Stop," she whispered in a shaky voice as she backed

away a fraction from the heat of his all-too-comfortable body.

"I don't want to stop," he coaxed huskily.

"Our company will be here any minute," she protested weakly as his mouth came back to reclaim hers.

"The hell with our company. Let's lock the door and go to bed," he growled in a low, sexy voice. "I'm going to make love to you."

"Mitch . . ." He was assaulting every fiber of her being now as his hands slipped down the front of her sundress and his fingers came in contact with the soft, velvet flesh of her breasts.

"Don't fight it, sweetheart, it's been so damn long since we've been together. . . ." He buried his face in the fragrance of her hair, and his embrace tightened painfully.

Shannon knew how utterly crazy this was, but at the moment, her mind was in a state of limbo. It had been so long since he had made love to her. She longed to feel him lying next to her, to experience his passionate lovemaking once more, and to hear him whisper all the things she longed to hear, if only for one night.

Mitch tilted her face up to meet his, and her eyes told him all he needed to know. "Come here, angel," he murmured, reaching down to pick her up in his arms. Their mouths met eagerly again as he carried her through the kitchen toward his bedroom.

The sound of the doorbell barely penetrated their passion-drugged senses as Mitch placed her on his bed and lay down on top of her. Their kisses were hot and urgent as the doorbell peeled impatiently.

"Mitch . . . the door," Shannon murmured.

"Forget it," he rasped, burying his face in the valley of her breasts.

"We can't forget it," she argued as the sound of the doorbell broke the silence again. "They know we're in here!"

Mitch slumped against her in defeat, muttering a disgusted expletive under his breath. "Shannon . . . honey, I need you so much," he pleaded, his mouth mingling sweetly with hers. "If we stop right now, I know we'll go right back to our old stubborn ways. . . ."

Shannon pushed him aside and sat up slowly, straightening her dress with shaky fingers. "Maybe it's for the best, Mitch. I don't know what got into me. . . ."

"I know what got into *me,* dammit! I need you, Shannon!"

"You don't need me, Mitch, you just need a woman," she accused tearfully as she slid off the bed and pushed her hair back into order. "We have got to answer the door!" she snapped as a loud pounding erupted outside.

"All right! Maybe I do need a woman," he conceded angrily as he fumbled with his own clothing, "but you can't tell me you weren't all for the idea!"

"I'm not telling you anything, except you are going to answer that door and let your dinner guests in!" she spouted irritably. "I'm sure your 'date' will be more than happy to fill your needs!"

Mitch's face turned dark and wrathful. "Now, that's the best idea you've had all day! I'm sure she'd be more than happy to!" He turned and stalked heatedly out of the bedroom.

Shannon sank back down on the bed and let the tears fall freely. Now she had deliberately sent him into that siren's welcoming arms!

It took several minutes for her to regain control of her

shattered emotions and join Mitch and their guests in the other room.

Cliff Webster stood as Shannon entered the room, a broad smile on his face. "There you are!" he greeted merrily.

"Hi, Cliff." Her eyes fell on the redhead draped over the chair Mitch was sitting in, and her stomach tensed. "Hello, Rhonda."

Rhonda acknowledged Shannon's greeting with a nod of her head. Since learning that the Wranebows were divorced, all pretense of friendship had been tossed aside between the two women.

Mitch eyed Shannon coldly, then rose from his chair and walked over to the small bar he had set up. "Sangria anyone?"

"That sounds nice." Rhonda followed Mitch over to the bar and accepted the glass he held out for her.

Cliff walked over and escorted Shannon to the small bar. "This is nice," he agreed as he handed Shannon her drink. "How is the business coming along?"

"Just fine," Shannon said with a sincere smile. Mitch and she had finally been able to bring everything under control, and the resort was running very smoothly at the moment.

"I stopped by Jerry and Marla's room this afternoon. They are really improving more every day. Another couple of weeks should see them safely home," Cliff observed happily as he picked up his own drink. "Of course, they won't be able to do much for a while, but I think Jerry's going crazy just lying up there in the hospital."

"Yes." Shannon laughed. "He doesn't make a very good invalid. I know they'll both be happy to get home."

"I think I'll put the hamburgers on the grill," Mitch

127

announced, picking up his drink and walking toward the kitchen area to gather up the things he needed.

"I'll be glad to help," Rhonda offered, hurriedly trailing along behind him.

"Thanks, Rhonda, but why don't you stay here and visit with Shannon. Cliff can keep me company." Mitch glanced at Shannon pointedly. "Don't you agree that would be nice, Shannon?"

"Uh . . . oh . . . yes, that would be nice." Shannon avoided Mitch's penetrating gaze.

"Good. Come on, Cliff, you and I can visit while I get the meat started. The grill is out by the pool."

"Let's go with them," Rhonda told Shannon as the men were leaving the room.

"Oh . . . no . . . I don't think they want us to," Shannon hedged, trying to think of some way to lead Rhonda into a discussion of her ex-husband without seeming obvious. This was going to be a difficult topic of conversation. She had racked her brain all afternoon to come up with why she disliked Mitch so much, and suddenly realized that she actually had little about him to dislike. Other than the fact he stubbornly refused to give in to her demands about his job, he had been a very easy man to live with. He had been loving, supportive in any new adventure she tried, in a good mood most of the time. . . . It simply infuriated her when she was unable to come up with one bad thing to say about him!

"You like Mitch, don't you?" she blurted out tactlessly.

Rhonda turned from her position at the window to face Shannon in surprise. "I . . . well . . . yes, I think he's a very nice man."

"Oh, he is," Shannon agreed quickly. "Very . . . well, sort of nice."

"Look, Shannon. I feel rather strange knowing that you're his ex-wife, but he did ask me here for dinner this evening," she said defensively.

"Oh, my. Don't feel strange. Our marriage is over." Shannon willed her voice to remain calm. "He's free to date anyone he chooses."

"Well, I hope you don't mind me saying this, but I'm ecstatic that he chose me," Rhonda confided in a friend-lier tone than she had been using. "He is just about the best-looking man I've ever laid eyes on. All that dark curly hair, and those blue eyes . . . and those darling dimples . . ." Rhonda caught herself and looked at Shannon uneasily. "Well, you know what I mean . . ."

"Yeah," Shannon responded remorsefully, "I know what you mean. But all of that is just superficial. Deep down, he's a dirty rat."

Rhonda's eyes flew up to meet Shannon's. "A dirty rat?"

"A low-down, conniving dirty rat," Shannon amended.

Rhonda smiled tolerantly. "Of course *you* would say that. You're his ex-wife."

"No, this isn't just sour grapes on my part," Shannon argued with a serious face. "He can't be trusted."

"You mean he ran around on you?" Rhonda's eyes gleamed distrustfully.

"Every day of our marriage," Shannon affirmed sol-emnly with a long, drawn-out sigh. "I learned to live with it, but I always felt so sorry for all those . . . children he left in his wake." Shannon hung her head sadly. If that sucker wanted her to lay it on thick, then that's exactly what she would do!

"Children? He didn't say anything about having children," Rhonda mused thoughtfully. "How many does he have?"

"Seven, last time I counted. But that was months ago. . . ." She let her voice leave the implication there could be more by this time.

"Seven!" Rhonda was shocked.

"Or eight," Shannon persisted. She was beginning to enjoy this little deceit.

Rhonda was silent for a moment, then her full red lips broke apart in a wicked, sly grin. "That Mitchell must be quite a man."

Shannon's face fell as she realized she had only sweetened the prize for Rhonda.

"Oh . . . yes . . . yes, well he was until . . . the accident."

"Accident?" Rhonda's smile dropped off her face.

"Yes. . . ." Shannon searched her brain for some feasible story. "He suffered a job-related accident. He fell off . . . a ten-story building."

"And he lived to tell about it?" Rhonda gasped.

"It left a lot of scars . . . mentally," Shannon improvised. "After the fall, he was never able to . . . well, you know something as traumatic as that would naturally affect a person's life. The doctor says that someday he will probably resume a normal sex life . . . if you know what I mean." Shannon fibbed blatantly.

"Is that what broke up your marriage? The fall?" Rhonda inquired sympathetically.

"You could say that." Shannon gave a sigh of martyrdom. "Neither one of us could ever get that 'fall' out of our mind." At least that part wasn't a lie!

"Poor man," Rhonda mused pityingly. "Well, personally, I think all he needs is someone to lead him back into manhood. . . ." She caught her private thoughts and glanced at Shannon. "I think all he needs is a little time, and he'll be back to the strong, virile man he once was!" she amended tactfully.

"Oh, no! He's had therapy and all that rigamarole, Rhonda. . . ." Shannon began to grow uneasy. All these lies were backfiring on her, and she was only succeeding in making Mitch more desirable to Rhonda, instead of the opposite! "He's a hopeless case!" she emphasized.

"Nonsense. No man that good-looking and masculine is a hopeless case! If you ask me, all he needs is a woman willing to work with him. . . ."

"Nobody asked you!" Shannon shot back hatefully.

"Too bad, dearie. I'm taking it upon myself to help the poor man!" Rhonda planted her hands on her hips and glared at Shannon defiantly.

"All right, ladies, hamburgers will be ready in five minutes!" Mitch announced pleasantly as he walked into the room and surveyed the angry scene before him.

Rhonda rushed over and placed her arm around Mitch's and smiled up at him sweetly. "That sounds good. I'm starved."

Shannon's temper threatened to explode as she turned on her heel and stalked over to the kitchen area hoping to regain control of herself before she committed cold-blooded murder! That arrogant, revolting redhead!

In a few minutes Mitch joined her in the kitchen area. "Rhonda's outside. What in the hell is going on? I thought you were going to get her off my back!"

"I tried, you moron!"

"Don't start with me, Shannon! What went wrong? She's clinging to me like flypaper again!"

"I can't help it. I tried!" Shannon said, tears welling up in her eyes now. "She's determined to make a man out of you again." She sobbed.

"What!"

"She wants to make a man out of you again," Shannon repeated, tears streaming uncontrollably down her cheeks "and I have no doubt she'll work at it until she wears you down and she succeeds!"

Shannon whirled and ran out of the kitchen, leaving Mitch standing with his mouth open. She ran into her bedroom and slammed the door, falling across the bed miserably. Now, she had really done it! Rhonda would have Mitch in her bed before he could blink his eye. Not that he would protest overly much. As he said, he needed a woman, and Shannon had foolishly just handed him a hot-blooded redheaded one on a silver platter!

CHAPTER EIGHT

By the time Shannon returned from the bedroom, Mitch was on his way to see about her.

"Are you all right?"

"I'm just fine," she said coolly, trying to hide her red-rimmed eyes.

"Look, I don't know what went wrong, but we'll discuss it later. Our guests are sitting on the porch ready to eat, and I don't think we should keep them waiting," Mitch said shortly. He reached out and touched her flushed cheek. "Are you sure you're okay?"

"Don't worry about me." She shrugged off his finger in a petulant motion. "We don't want to keep *Rhonda* waiting."

"Now, wait a minute. I know you're hacked-off because she keeps throwing herself at me, but that's the point of this whole dinner. Didn't you tell her I was a bum?"

"I certainly did. And that was a stupid idea. I only succeeded in making things worse."

"How could you have made things worse? All you had to do was convince her I wasn't worth a plug nickel."

"I told her that." Shannon sniffed.

"And?"

"And, I added a few . . . little things of my own, but

133

it all sort of got out of hand, and by the time I was through, she was crazier than ever about you and your big blue eyes and cute little"—Shannon sniffed louder—"dimples!"

"My what?"

"Your damn little dimples!" she repeated curtly.

"Oh." He looked at her strangely. "But, what do my dimples got to do with anything?"

"It's not your 'dimples' she's worried about," Shannon confirmed irritably.

"Well, what in the hell is she worried about?" Mitch said in an exasperated voice.

"Your"—Shannon sniffed twice more—"inability to make love to a woman."

Mitch sank down in the nearest chair and stared at her blankly. "My what?"

"I told her you had had an accident and suffered tremendous mental anxiety and were no longer able to make love to a woman," Shannon explained in a patient voice, as if she were having to deal with an imbecile.

Mitch's eyes lost their blank look rapidly and replaced it with a look of pure violence. "Why in the hell did you tell her that?" he shouted.

"Shhh . . . they'll hear you." Shannon bounded over and placed her hand across Mitch's mouth. "Don't you see? I thought that would get her off your back pronto. What would she want with a man who couldn't . . . well . . . that was all I could think of at the moment!"

"Yumm mormmmm stupmmmm!" His voice filtered angrily through her clasped hand.

"I know, it was a stupid idea! Just pipe down!" She stared back into a pair of the most distressed blue eyes she had ever encountered. "If I take my hand off your mouth, will you be quiet?"

"Mcitysxzz!!" he sputtered.

Shannon let her hand drop away from his mouth.

"Why did you tell her that?" he demanded again in a harsh whisper.

"You told me I could tell her anything I wanted to," Shannon whispered back loudly. "That's all I could think of at the time!"

"Well, that's the lousiest bit of thinking you've ever come up with. Imagine! Me not being able to make love to a woman!" Mitch's eyes blazed indignantly.

"Yeah, just imagine! I'm sorry I've offended your manly, overinflated ego, but this was all your fault in the first place!" she reminded tensely. "Anyway, Rhonda's bound and determined she's going to correct that 'hang-up.'"

'What are we going to do?" Mitch slumped back in his chair miserably. "She'll never let up now."

"Can't you just tell her you're not interested!"

"Don't you think I've tried that? The crazy woman won't listen. My only other alternative is to start a fistfight with her, and I hardly think that's the gentlemanly way to do things!" Mitch pointed out sarcastically.

Shannon began to pace the floor in front of him, her mind springing into action. "All right, now let's not panic. There is a way out of this. Just give me a few minutes."

She whirled and snapped her fingers. "Tell her you have a communicable disease!"

Mitch glanced up in disgust. "How could I have a communicable disease if you just got through telling her I can't 'communicate' with anyone!"

Shannon's smile died a slow death. "Oh, yeah, I forgot about that. If we told her that, I'd have to admit I lied." She bit her lip thoughtfully. "Are you sure you don't want to stick to the accident story and try to fake it through until we can go home? We only have another two or three weeks?"

"Think of something else, Shannon!" he warned in an ominous tone of voice.

Shannon frowned. Well, there was one other thing she could do, but it would have to be as a last resort.

"All right, I do know of one other thing," she relented.

"What is it?" Mitch sat up straighter.

"But," she cautioned, "you'll have to make me a promise first."

"Okay, okay, what do you want?"

"I want you to stop this asinine matchmaking between me and Cliff Webster," she said firmly.

Mitch's grin was sly. "What's the matter? Don't you like your little *safe* buddy?"

"I neither like, nor dislike, Cliff. Regardless of what I feel for him, it is none of your business, and I want you to keep your nose out of it. Do you understand?"

"If that's what you want," he agreed smoothly. "I must admit, it wasn't doing anything for me to sit and watch him pant over you like a Siberian husky on a hot summer day. Now," he said as he rubbed his hands together enticingly, "what's the plan to get rid of the redhead?"

"You leave that to me. You just remember your promise. No more matchmaking."

"I promise." He grinned angelically. "Why don't you admit it, sweetheart, you're just a little jealous of Rhonda?"

136

"In a pig's eye," she scoffed. "I'm only doing this because you're so pitiful."

Mitch's grin was doubtful as he rose from the chair. "Bull! Bull! And double bull!"

"Watch your mouth, Wranebow. You're not off the hook yet," Shannon warned as they walked out on the porch to join their guests.

Shannon was sure that Cliff and Rhonda must have wondered what had happened to their host and hostess, but if they did, they showed no signs of impatience. Rhonda immediately latched on to Mitch for the rest of the evening, and Shannon was paired off with Cliff. Several times during the evening she saw Mitch frown as Cliff would casually drape his arm around her waist or lean over to carry on an intimate conversation with her. Shannon's own gaze never strayed far from her ex-husband, seething anew each time the redhead put her hands somewhere Shannon disapproved of. Which, in her opinion, happened most of the time!

As the evening dragged on, Shannon grew madder by the minute when she thought of why they were in this mess in the first place. If it hadn't been for Mitch, they could be enjoying a nice quiet evening together instead of trying to entertain two people whom neither one of them cared to be with!

It was with tremendous relief at the end of the evening when Shannon finally managed to get Rhonda alone and tell her the new story she had concocted as a last-ditch effort to save her ex-husband from the clutches of this depraved carrottop!

It was a sad Rhonda who took her leave a few minutes later, casting one last suspicious glance in Mitch's direction.

But it was an elated Mitch who closed the door, then scooped Shannon up in his arms and swung her around the room happily. "I don't know what you told her, but it worked! She made a point of telling me that if things didn't work out to call her. She even gave me her home phone number!"

"When is she leaving?" Shannon asked excitedly.

"I think she's going to stay on another week or so, but at least she'll be off my back." He grinned with relief.

"If you ask me, she wasn't half the burden you seem to imply," Shannon said curtly.

Mitch held her out away from him so he could face her. "I knew it! You are jealous!"

"I am not!" Shannon denied crossly.

"You are too! And"—he grinned smugly—"I planned it that way."

Shannon looked at him in disbelief. "You what?"

Mitch shrugged. "I planned it this way. I figured you cared more than you were letting on. You would have never gone to the trouble to get rid of Rhonda unless you still cared just a tiny bit."

"You . . ." she sputtered.

"Stop sputtering and kiss me, you fool." His lips captured hers easily. When they broke apart minutes later, Shannon had to admit he had a point.

"Are you mad?" he asked, brushing his lips against her hair as he gave her a tight squeeze.

Mad wasn't quite the word Shannon would have used, but for the moment she decided to be docile.

"Not really. I'm just tired. Rhonda didn't take the news of our reconciliation very well."

Mitch kissed her again lazily. "Is that what you told her? That we were getting back together?"

"It's the only thing I could think of to make her give up the chase permanently. It was no easy job though. I had just told her earlier the marriage was over."

"How did you cover that?"

"I told her I had lied to her. Which I had. But not about that."

"Well, whatever you did, I'm grateful." He kissed her again sweetly.

"Just as long as you remember that it was only a deterrent."

"How can I forget?" he grumbled.

"Just to make sure you don't—" She picked up a glass still filled with sangria and dumped it over his head angrily.

Mitch reared back and looked at her in disbelief. She tranquilly set the glass back down and wiped her sticky hands on the front of his shirt. "From now on, Mitchell," she began patiently, "don't try to matchmake, or make me jealous, ever again. It upsets me."

Casting one last, withering glance in his direction, she exited the kitchen, leaving him standing in the living room with sangria dripping off his ears in rivulets.

The war of silence lasted longer than usual this time. It was a full week before either Mitch or Shannon spoke to each other. Mitch stayed in his part of the room, and Shannon stayed in hers. As the week wore on, the silence put a strain on Shannon's already frayed nerves. It didn't help in the least that Rhonda was still lurking in the shadows waiting for some small sign that the Wranebows' intended reconciliation was a mistake.

Why couldn't Rhonda be a poor divorcée who had to watch every penny instead of a rich one who could afford to spend the entire summer lolling around the lake looking for a man? Shannon thought irritably as she peeked out of the kitchen window and watched Mitch chat with Rhonda as he put the chemicals in the resort's pool. As usual, Rhonda's bathing suit was barely under the wire of decency, and Shannon watched irritably as the redhead paraded around the pool in front of Mitch.

With a resigned sigh, she walked over to the table and sat down. Laying her head on her arms, she rested for a moment, wishing she was back home.

In a few minutes she decided to call her office and see how things were going. Twenty minutes of conversation with Molly improved her outlook considerably, and by the time Mitch finished his chores and came back in the house, she was ready to fly the truce flag.

"Want to eat dinner with me tonight?" she asked casually, just as if they had been carrying on a pleasant conversation instead of a cold war for the last week.

Mitch glanced up at her as he was taking off his work boots, then turned around and looked behind him. Turning back around to face her, he asked cautiously, "Were you talking to *me?*"

"Who else is in the room?"

"No one. But I was under the impression we were having another fight."

"We were," she said politely.

Mitch resumed pulling off his boots. "I gather we're not now?"

"It's up to you," she replied defensively, putting him in a bad light if he chose to refuse her gracious offer.

"What are we having to eat?" With those simple words he accepted her cease-fire diplomatically.

Shannon released an inaudible sigh. "I don't know. I'll look in the refrigerator and come up with something."

"I'm going to take a quick shower," Mitch grumbled, picking up his shoes and heading for the bathroom.

By the time he returned, Shannon had dinner on the stove.

Mitch inhaled appreciatively and walked over to where she was standing at the stove. "Smells good. What is it?"

"Just some minute steaks and vegetables. I'm not too good a cook . . . you know."

"Yes . . . I know," he said bluntly. Lifting up one of the lids to a small saucepan, his eyes grew round as he looked at the slimy concoction. "Holeeee Moses!" He let out a low whistle between his teeth. "What in the hell is that?"

Shannon peered curiously into the pan. "Okra. Why?"

"What do you do with it?" he asked, still awed by the blurping, bubbling mass.

"Eat it, stupid!"

Mitch looked at her incredulously. "You may eat it! I don't even want it on the table with me! It looks like a pan of slugs!"

A trail of black smoke belched out of the skillet the steak was frying in as they stood there arguing over the okra.

"Now look what you made me do!" Shannon yelled, grabbing the skillet off the stove and throwing it into the sink. The kitchen was thick with the black smoke as she ran water over the flaming steaks.

Mitch folded his arms and leaned against the sink, his face a mask of disappointment. "Well, back to square one."

141

Shannon wiped a stray hair out of her face and leaned against the sink. "What are we going to do now?"

"We could go out," Mitch offered.

"No." Shannon sank down in a chair. "I don't want to have to get cleaned up to go out."

They both fell silent for a moment. Finally, Mitch sighed. "I'll fix our supper. What do you want?"

Shannon glanced up at him gratefully. "Anything you'd like to fix."

Mitch wrinkled his nose in distaste at the thought of cooking, but he had made the offer. Much to his surprise, the meal turned out delicious.

Later, Mitch was sprawled out on the couch smoking one of his cheroots as Shannon finished what few dishes they had used. Their meal had been pleasant as they both relaxed and discussed the day they had just spent.

"Hey, hurry up in there."

Shannon dried the last cup and put the dish towel on the rack. Rubbing hand lotion on her hands, she wandered over the chalk line into his territory.

"Why?"

"I thought we might play some cards." Mitch sat up on the sofa and put his cigar in the ash tray. "How about it?"

Shannon shrugged. It was obvious she didn't have anything better to do at the moment. "What kind?"

"Poker, or whatever you'd like," he offered courteously.

"Poker sounds like fun."

"Good." Mitch stuck the cheroot back between his teeth and reached for a deck of cards. "Five card draw?"

She nodded her silent approval and reached for the box of matches to use as poker chips.

Mitch dealt the hand smoothly, and for the next hour they played quietly. By the time Shannon had won five hands, she was truly amazed at her ability to defeat Mitch, who had always been an excellent poker player.

"Do you want to keep playing the same thing?" she asked perkily as she dealt out another hand.

Mitch leaned back and squinted through his cigar smoke at her. "Where did you learn to play poker like that?"

Shannon lifted her shoulders. "I really don't know." It surprised her as much as it did him. "I guess I'm just a natural." She smiled smugly.

"Yeah." Mitch leaned forward and picked up his cards. "I suppose that's possible. But I think the reason you're slaughtering me is because I'm used to playing for higher stakes."

"Oh, ho! Stop making flimsy excuses. Can't you just admit I'm beating you fair and square?" she chided, sorting through her cards confidently.

"Maybe so," he mused, studying his hand earnestly. "But I think we could make the game more interesting."

Shannon glanced over at him. "What? Money?"

Mitch shook his head negatively. "No. That's not interesting enough."

"Blood?" she teased playfully, upping the stakes.

Mitch sat up straighter and took a long drag off his cheroot and exhaled a chain of tiny smoke rings. "No, I was thinking of something much more interesting."

Laying her cards face down on the table, she crossed her hands patiently. "You name it." She was feeling extremely competent about meeting any challenge he would issue.

An ornery grin spread across his face. "I don't think you'd have the nerve to play for the odds I'd suggest," he drawled.

"Oh, really? What odds do you have in mind?" she countered smoothly.

His blue eyes ran lazily over her feminine curves, pausing suggestively on the neckline of her thin cotton blouse.

"Let's play a friendly game of strip poker," he suggested calmly.

An avalanche of emotions played across Shannon's pretty features, ranging from surprise, to disbelief, to simmering anger. Clearing her throat nervously, she uncrossed her hands and picked up her cards impassively. "That sounds interesting." Her brown eyes met his blue ones defiantly. "I'll take two cards please."

"Two cards for the little lady in blue," Mitch said lightly, dealing her two new cards. "And, the gentleman will take three."

Shannon covered a sly smile. He was already off to a bad start!

A couple of minutes later Shannon laid down a flush, easily beating Mitch's three jacks.

"Sorry." She smiled serenely.

Mitch reached up to unbutton his shirt, taking the defeat in unruffled stride. "That's the way the cookie crumbles," he acknowledged as he shrugged out of the shirt and threw it on the sofa. "Your deal."

Seconds later they each had a new hand of cards.

"How many?" Shannon asked pleasantly.

"Three." Mitch studied his hand through a veil of spiraling smoke.

"Three for the little gentleman with the bare chest," Shannon mocked. "And, the lady, fully dressed in blue, takes one."

Picking up her new card, Shannon's heart leaped as she saw the deuce she needed to complete a full house. "I'll bet four matchsticks!" she said excitedly, forgetting for the moment to play it cool.

"Four?" Mitch looked thoughtful as he drummed his fingers on the table absently. "Okay. I'll see yours and raise you two."

"Two?"

Mitch threw six matchsticks on the mounting pile. "Two," he confirmed in a steady voice.

"All right, I'll see your two and call."

She smiled inwardly as two more sticks fell on the pile. She could sit here and raise him all night, but she wanted to give the poor fool a break.

Mitch's grin was cocky as he laid his cards face up on the table. "Okay, little lady dressed fully in blue, I have four of a kind," he said calmly.

Shannon frowned, then swallowed uneasily. "That beats a full house, doesn't it?"

"Afraid so." He leaned back and lit a new cheroot.

Reaching down, Shannon slipped off her sandals and handed them to Mitch. "I'm tired now. I think I want to quit."

"I think not," he said firmly. "You agreed to play, and you're not backing out just because you lost one lousy hand."

"Well, just one more hand," she relented hesitantly. She knew she would never live it down if she quit now.

Thirty minutes later she would have given anything if she had followed her original plan. Suddenly Mitch had turned pro once more, and she was down to her panties and bra.

"Royal flush," Mitch announced jubilantly as he laid his winning hand on the table and smiled wickedly at Shannon.

She slammed her losing hand down on the table and jumped up. "You are cheating!" she accused angrily.

"I am not!" Mitch stood up to face her. "You're just a sore loser."

"You can say that because you're not the one standing here nearly in the buff," she flared.

"My shirt's off," he reasoned nicely.

"Big deal!"

The smile disappeared slowly from Mitch's face as his eyes surveyed her nearly nude body.

She watched warily as desire took the place of amusement on his face. "Mitch . . ." she said nervously as she started backing slowly away from the card table.

"Come here, Shannon," he said quietly.

"No, I think this has gone far enough."

"No, it hasn't." He held his hand out to her. "Come here to me," he repeated firmly.

Her footsteps faltered as her gaze met his. "We both know what will happen if I do, Mitch, and I don't want it to happen. Nothing's changed between us."

"Come here, Shannon," he repeated, only this time she snapped to attention at the no-nonsense tone in his voice.

"I don't want to. I'm afraid," she whispered.

"All right. Then, I'll come to you." He started forward cautiously. "You don't need to be afraid of me. We both want this, you know that."

Shannon shook her head as he slowly approached her. "It's not fair. You know how you make me feel, and it

146

isn't right to take advantage of my weaknesses," she argued softly. "I'm . . . I'm not even on the pill anymore, Mitch!"

"I'll take care of things," he promised quietly. "You just come here."

He reached her side and placed his hands on her hips, drawing her up close to the proof of his overpowering need of her. "You forget I have my weaknesses too, Shannon, and I think we're both tired of denying them."

The feel of his bare chest against the sheer fabric of her bra sent waves of longing through her. He was right. They both had denied themselves for too long the pleasure that they knew was awaiting them.

Involuntarily, her hands crept up around his neck, and she lifted her face for the kiss that she knew she wasn't going to refuse. For a moment they gazed at each other, drinking in the familiar touch and smell of each other.

"No matter what happened between us, you have always been something very special to me." He kissed her softly, his breath mingling sweetly with hers. "You've always been my special girl."

Tears sprang to Shannon's eyes as she returned the kiss, drawing herself closer to his comforting presence. Her hands moved restlessly in the dark hair on his chest, eager to know his body once more.

"You said you hadn't been with another woman since the divorce. Were you telling the truth?" she whispered hopefully.

Burying his face in her hair, he sighed. "I'm not going to lie to you, sweetheart. There were a couple of times that I tried to make love to another woman, but I'm afraid both times were complete flops. Once, I was so drunk I didn't even know my name; another time I was so damn lonely I thought I was going to lose my mind. I took a woman I used to know to a motel. She was the one that backed out when I kept calling her Shannon."

Shannon's hand reached down to undo the belt on his jeans. "If you expect me to say I'm sorry, you'll be waiting a long time," she told him with relief shining brightly in her eyes.

"I don't expect you to say anything," he murmured, bringing his mouth back down to meet hers hungrily. "I just want you to let me make love to you. Tomorrow, you can call me anything you want, throw things at me, accuse me of the vilest of deeds, but for tonight"—he reached down and lifted her up in his arms—"just for tonight, we're going to bury the past and spend hours making love."

He carried her to his bedroom, exchanging smoldering kisses with her along the way. As he laid her on the bed, he finished slipping out of his clothes before he slid on top of her. Moments later her bra and lacy panties joined his clothes on the floor.

He sucked in his breath as their naked bodies merged against each other, his hand gripping tightly in her hair as his lips devoured hers with insatiable kisses, his tongue searching out the sweet recesses of her mouth.

She moaned quietly as he moved suggestively against her, drawing her tighter into his embrace.

"I've missed you," he rasped huskily as his hand took hers to touch him more intimately. His breathing grew ragged as she eagerly stroked him lovingly.

"I know, and I've missed you too," she admitted with a small whimper. And she had. At times the pain of losing him had been nearly unbearable.

Mitch rolled over on his back, taking her with him as

their kisses grew more urgent and their hands greedily reacquainted themselves with each other's bodies, sighing with pleasure as they both remembered the things that were the most pleasing to each other.

"This doesn't make any difference to our situation, Mitch," she warned in a helpless whisper. "You still have that horrible job. . . ."

One large hand came up to close over her mouth gently. "We're not going to talk about that damn job tonight." His mouth again claimed hers persuasively.

Mitch's large frame trembled as he slid on top of her once more, murmuring words of intimacy in her ear as he joined with her passionately, sending them soaring into a world of oblivion, aware only of each other and the overpowering need to assuage their hungry bodies.

They made love with an urgency that could only culminate much sooner than either wanted. As they reached the top in unison, Mitch moaned and poured out his love for her in strong, powerful thrusts, sending them spiraling into joyous fulfillment.

The room grew silent as he collapsed in her arms and they drifted back to reality slowly. In the lazy afterglow of their lovemaking, it was hard for Shannon to realize that the last few minutes had only been the needs of a man and woman who had too long denied their own bodies. Memories of when she and Mitch had been married flooded her mind, causing the tears that she had held tightly in check to begin to trickle slowly down her cheeks. They splashed on Mitch's bare shoulder as his embrace tightened almost painfully.

"Don't cry," he pleaded in a muffled tone.

"I can't help it," she murmured, burying her face in his broad chest.

"Are you sorry?" he asked softly.

"No, at least not about our making love," she whispered.

"Then, what are you crying about?" he asked tenderly, kissing her forehead.

She wanted to tell him she was crying because she was a woman who didn't know what she wanted. She longed to hear him tell her that he loved her and together they would find a way back to happiness. But he hadn't said any of those things to her. Only that he wanted to make love to her.

"I don't know why," she answered lamely.

"Yes, you do," he said quietly, rolling back over and pulling her on top of his broad chest. "You're crying for the same reason I want to."

Her serious brown eyes met his beautiful sad blue ones. "I'm crying because I wish things could be different," she finally admitted.

"They could be," he murmured, his voice breaking.

Shannon reached up and gently traced the tears that slid quietly down his cheeks now with her finger, her own tears increasing. "Don't you cry," she pleaded. But they both knew that now that the tears had started there would be no stopping them.

They lay in the dark, quiet room and cried together, letting all the pent-up disappointments and painful emotions that had filled their lives for the last year come flooding out. Their salty tears mingled with their kisses as they talked quietly about all the things that had torn them apart in the last few months.

"You know there's a more painful way to lose someone than just death," Mitch pointed out when Shannon repeatedly brought up his hazardous job.

150

"Just death!" she exclaimed disbelievingly.

"You know what I mean," he cautioned. "What we've gone through the last year . . . well, I don't know about you, but death would have been easier for me."

Shannon laid her head back down on his chest, silently contemplating his words. Funny, but she was about to come to that same conclusion herself.

It was very late when they finally fell asleep in each other's arms, their problems no closer to a solution than a year ago.

CHAPTER NINE

The next morning Shannon rose early and made their breakfast. When Mitch walked into the kitchen, he took her in his arms and kissed her good morning, making it clear that he would rather go back to bed with her than eat the lovely breakfast she had prepared for him.

"Aren't you the one who is always complaining about your meals?" she teased, matching his kisses eagerly.

"That was before I could have you for breakfast," he murmured suggestively as his hands indecently explored beneath her nightgown.

"I don't believe I heard you knock," she said primly, kissing him lingeringly as her hands buried in the thick, lustrous hair on his chest.

Mitch groaned and glanced down at the floor. "I am over my line, aren't I . . . hey! Where's the chalk line?"

Shannon smiled smugly and pulled his mouth back to meet hers. "Gone. You no longer need an invitation to enter my side of the house," she said warmly.

"Well, hallelujah! What brought that on?" he asked with a broad grin.

Shrugging her shoulders, she strolled over to pour his coffee. "Aren't you glad?"

"You bet I am," he said sincerely as he took the cup she offered and set it back down on the table. "I can't tell you how much I appreciate it, but I can sure show you." He scooped her up in his arms and carried her over to the sofa, kissing her deeply as he walked.

"I never remember you being insatiable," she teased as she playfully bit his ear.

"Then your memory is doing you a gross injustice," he drawled wickedly as his hands slipped her negligee off her shoulders and he began to kiss her along her satin neckline. "What are you doing with clothes on?"

"It is broad daylight," she reminded primly as she arched closer to his plundering mouth.

"Yeah, I'd noticed." He grinned, drawing back away from her to survey the lush curves he had bared for his lusty observation. He let out a low, appreciative whistle. "Wow, I'd forgotten how well you were built, Mrs. Wranebow."

"It's still Ms. Murphy, and you're not bad yourself, fella," she whispered, running her hands over the taut muscles of his arms and shoulders. "And speaking of clothes, look who's overdressed now."

"I thought you preferred me to wear clothes. At least I seemed to recall a day when you made me put a shirt on, or else!"

"You're free to run around half-naked in front of *me*, no one else." She pulled his head down and kissed him suggestively, running her tongue softly inside his mouth.

"You keep kissing me like that, and we'll be here all day," he warned, running his hand down the inside of her leg seductively.

"So? Who's in a hurry?"

"Now who's the insatiable one?"

Her hand slowly trailed down the broadness of his chest, pausing to gently stroke him pleasurably as her kisses answered his question long before she actually spoke. "I am."

"Are both the doors locked?" he murmured as she helped him slip his tennis shorts and briefs off.

"I think so. Doors all locked, blinds all pulled." She kissed his ear then whispered something low and intimate to him.

"Oh, lady," he said huskily, "there should be a law against what you're doing to me right now."

"I wouldn't vote in favor of it," she murmured huskily, sliding on top of his large frame.

"Who in their right mind would?" he groaned, as they came together in an explosion of hot searing passion. Words faded as they made love in a hungry, urgent manner. A year's separation from each other had left them both in a ravenous mood for the other. Only too soon, the aching pressure mounted unbearably, then exploded into blissful, shattering fulfillment.

It was another hour, and another round of spontaneous lovemaking, before they found themselves eating a cold breakfast and giggling like two teenagers. The phone rang, interrupting yet another stolen kiss between them.

Mitch went to answer it as Shannon cleared the breakfast dishes off the table.

When he returned ten minutes later, he sneaked up behind her and put his arms around her waist, nuzzling her neck lovingly. "That was Mom."

"Oh? Is anything wrong?"

"No, she's fine. She wants to come down a few days when Marla and Jerry are released."

"That's next weekend," Shannon mused thoughtfully as she ran hot dishwater into the sink.

"Yeah, I told her to come on down, there would be plenty of room for all of us here."

Shannon moved out of his embrace and wiped off the table. "Huh-uh. Not all of us," she corrected. "You'll have to rent a room in one of the motels around here, since all the cottages are taken and there are only two bedrooms and a hide-a-bed in this house."

"So? Mom can have the guest room, and you and I will take the hide-a-bed," he said reasonably.

"*We* are not taking the hide-a-bed, Mitch!"

"Why not?" He looked like she had slapped his hands after finding them in the cookie jar.

"I thought that we agreed that last night didn't change anything," she pointed out patiently. "I'm not going to deny that I want to be with you these last few days before Marla and Jerry come home, but we still have so many things to discuss."

Mitch blocked her words with an impatient kiss. "All right. But let's give ourselves this week together before we make any decisions," he coaxed gently.

Shannon smiled and ran her fingers through his thick, curly hair. "You know, Rhonda's right."

Mitch frowned. "About what?"

"You *do* have the cutest dimples and blue eyes I've ever seen on a man."

"Oh, come on, Shannon." Mitch's face flushed a dark crimson.

"But you do," she persisted, lovingly kissing each dimple as she talked. "And it should be against the law for a man to have eyelashes like you do."

"If you're talking about the length of them, you're right. It should be against the law! They're too damn long. I took the scissors and cut them all off when I was a kid."

"You didn't." Shannon laughed.

"I certainly did," he confirmed heatedly.

"They're beautiful," she praised, moving back to kiss each eye affectionately.

"You think so, huh? Well, if you like those stupid eyelashes so much, I have something else you're probably going to be crazy about," he teased, pulling her closer to his taut thighs.

"Mitch," she scolded. "You can't be serious!"

"Afraid so," he grinned wickedly. "I'll teach you to tell wild stories to pushy redheads about my sex drive," he threatened as he picked her up in his arms and carried her over to the sofa.

"I'm not a bit repentant." She giggled as his mouth covered hers hungrily.

The remaining days they spent together were ideal to both of them. Although the days were still filled with hard work, Shannon's nights were now filled with love. No longer did they try to deny their overpowering attraction to each other, nor did they even want to.

It would all be over soon, Shannon kept reminding herself as the days sped by swiftly. The divorce had not been mentioned since the night they had tried to talk things out and failed. They seemed to exist in a world where only today counted, but Shannon knew that that could not go on forever.

Before she knew it, it was the Friday before Labor Day, and Mitch had gone to the hospital to pick up Marla and Jerry while she stayed home to welcome his mother.

Katherine Wranebow arrived before the others, bringing with her a cheerful smile and a loving hug for Shannon.

"It's so good to see you again, dear," she murmured as she hugged her ex-daughter-in-law tightly. "I have worried about you so much."

"I'm doing fine, Mom," Shannon assured her as she led her into the kitchen for a cup of coffee before Mitch returned. She had always called Mitch's mother Mom.

"Well, I'm glad you are. I don't think Mitch is, but he would never let me know that." Katherine sighed as she sat down at the table.

"I know, he never was one to let his feelings be known," Shannon agreed, although she had to admit silently to herself that that was not quite true. Mitch had been very open about his feelings the last few weeks, but as yet he had not told her he still loved her and wanted to remarry. And, if he did, what would her answer be?

While they waited for the other half of the Wranebow family to return, they chatted about impersonal things, avoiding the touchy subject of Mitch and Shannon's divorce. Before they knew it, they heard Mitch's car pulling into the driveway.

Settling the injured Wranebows proved to be easily taken care of. Jerry and Marla were quickly put to bed in their own room, where tears of happiness could be seen in Marla's eyes as she settled back blissfully on her pillow and closed her eyes. "Do you know how wonderful it is to be back in my own home?" she asked in a voice breaking with emotion.

Even though Jerry's leg was still in a cast, he managed to reach over and hold his wife close. "I think I just might, pretty lady," he teased affectionately. For a moment they looked at each other, the pain and anguish of the last few weeks mirrored sadly in their eyes.

Mitch took Shannon's hand and led her out of the bedroom, giving Jerry and Marla the first real privacy they had experienced in a very long time.

"Do they need anything?" Katherine asked as she glanced up from the salad she was cutting up for the evening meal.

"No, they're both just fine," Shannon assured her as she slapped a carrot out of Mitch's hand.

"Hey!" He grinned, then reached for a cucumber. "Knock off the rough stuff. I'll tell my mom on you!"

"Go ahead," Shannon teased as she bit into the carrot herself.

Mitch winked at her and backed out the door. Even though Marla and Jerry were back home, there was still a lot of work to be done.

By evening Mitch and Shannon were tired, but happy, as they joined Katherine in Jerry and Marla's bedroom to eat dinner on TV trays.

"Say, by the way," Jerry said between forkfuls of roast beef, "I forgot to mention this on the way home, but Cliff was able to find us an older couple to run the resort for the next few weeks, or at least until one of us gets back on our feet."

Mitch glanced at his brother in surprise. "I thought you couldn't afford to hire anyone."

Jerry looked momentarily disconcerted as his fork paused in midair. "Oh . . . yeah . . . well . . ."

"Oh, we couldn't . . . can't," Marla broke in hurriedly, "but this happens to be an old retired couple who will work very cheaply. They've been gone all summer and only returned yesterday."

Shannon looked at her sister suspiciously. For the first time it occurred to her that Marla and Jerry might have taken advantage of a tragic situation to do a little match-making of their own.

Marla smiled sheepishly at her sister, then hurriedly turned her attention back to her meal.

"So, I guess you and Shannon are free to resume your normal lives after the holiday," Jerry continued.

Shannon's stomach suddenly turned queasy as she realized this was the moment she had been dreading for the last week. She pushed her plate back and sipped her tea thoughtfully.

From the corner of her eye she noticed that Mitch's plate had gone almost untouched, as he stood and lit one of his cheroots and walked over to stare moodily out the window.

"You've hardly touched your dinner, dear," Katherine said as she watched Mitch smoke his cigar in thoughtful silence.

"I'm not hungry, Mom," he replied absently.

When the dishes were cleared away, they played cards together for the rest of the evening. Neither Shannon nor Mitch could keep their mind on the game. More than once they found themselves gazing at each other. Yet, when it was time for Mitch to leave for his motel room, he didn't single her out to say good night. Instead, he said good night to the group as a whole, then went out to his car alone.

While Katherine helped Jerry into the bathroom, Shannon straightened the sheets on the bed and fluffed Marla's pillow. "Can you think of anything you need?"

"No, nothing." Marla stretched contentedly. "I have everything in the world I want!"

Shannon smiled but said nothing. Wouldn't it be wonderful to have everything in the world you wanted? she thought enviously.

Marla caught the sad expression on her sister's face and reached out a comforting hand. "How about you? Are you any happier now?"

Shannon sank down on the bed tiredly. "Not really," she admitted with a soft sigh.

"Mitch?"

Shannon nodded miserably.

"I'd rather hoped that the last few weeks would have made you both see that the divorce had been a mistake," Marla mused absently.

A set of serious brown eyes focused accusingly on her. "Did you hatch up this fiasco in hopes of getting Mitch and me back together?"

Marla looked surprised, then disgusted. "Oh, you guessed! I remember telling Jerry the night of the accident, 'Jerry, let's go out and get ourselves nearly killed so we can try and get Shannon and Mitch to come to their senses'! Naturally, he jumped right up and complimented me on such an original plot and reached for the car keys."

"Marla! I didn't mean it that way," Shannon scolded with a touch of pink in her cheeks, "I merely meant that it seemed rather suspicious when I finally stopped to think about it. It's unlikely that you and Jerry wouldn't have the money to hire someone to take care of the resort. You two seem like you're doing okay financially."

It was Marla's turn for her cheeks to turn rosy. "Oh . . . that. Well, it was all Jerry's idea at first. He mentioned it in the emergency room, and at the time, I was in too much pain and too worried about him to disagree.

160

Later, I really thought about it and decided it was worth a try."

"I wish you two would have kept out of it!" Shannon said gently.

"It didn't work?" Marla peered at Shannon anxiously.

"Not in the way you were hoping for," Shannon disclosed unhappily. "All it's done is complicate matters."

"Well," Marla sighed, "at least we tried."

Shannon patted her sister's hand reassuringly. "I appreciate what you tried to do, but Mitch and I have a very serious problem. I can't live with his profession, and he won't give it up."

"That is just plain stubbornness on your part, Shannon. I know that Mitch is more than willing to give up the dangerous part of his profession when this job is finished. You have let your fears override your happiness."

"I can't help it!" Shannon defended herself.

"Yes, you can. You are going to have to work at having faith that everything will work out in the end. Can you honestly say that you've been happier this past year without Mitch than you would have been with him?"

"No," she conceded softly.

"Can you honestly say you don't love him?" Marla persisted.

"No."

"Am I being unreasonable to suggest that you have made a mistake and just won't admit it—even to yourself?"

The silence in the room was ominous as Shannon mulled the question over in her mind. Had she made an irreversible mistake by demanding that Mitch give up his job at the time he most needed her love and encouragement? Slowly the indisputable truth began to unfold be-

161

fore her. She *had* made a mistake. She had been demanding and completely unreasonable about his profession and had then compounded that mistake by childishly ordering him to see things her way—or forfeit the marriage. Mitch's tense words came back to her as she rose and walked over to the window. *"I never really thought you were serious about the divorce until the papers were served." "I never thought you were serious . . ." "I never thought you were serious . . ."*

Shannon turned from the window, tears cascading down her cheeks. "He didn't think I was serious about the divorce."

"I don't think you were, either," Marla said softly. "I think your divorce was a sad case of terminal bullheadedness!"

"Oh, Marla, do you think it's too late for me to correct that foolish mistake?"

"It's never too late." Marla laughed. "Now, wipe those tears out of your eyes and go after him, silly!"

Through tears of laughter and relief, Shannon leaned over and hugged her sister gratefully. "Don't expect me back tonight."

"I won't." Marla giggled. "And, have fun!"

"Oh, try to make up some excuse for Katherine," Shannon mumbled as she glanced in the mirror at her hair and makeup. "I don't know what you'll tell her . . ."

"How about the truth?" Katherine laughed as she led Jerry back into the bedroom.

Shannon froze, then turned around to face Mitch's mother. "Oh, Mom, I didn't mean . . ." Her cheeks colored with embarrassment.

"Will you just hush up and get out of here?" Katherine

shooed Shannon toward the door. "For the first time in my life, I'm giving a woman my blessing to take advantage of one of my boys!"

"I love all of you," Shannon called out gratefully as she was shoved through the doorway.

She ran into the kitchen and withdrew a package of weiners from the refrigerator and marshmallows from the cabinet, then bounded out the back door. Praying that Mitch would still be up, she drove to the motel Mitch was staying in, rehearsing over and over in her mind what she would say. She would let him know, discreetly, of course, that she had made a mistake, leaving the door open for him to apologize for his stubbornness, and ask her to remarry him. Naturally, she would accept his proposal, but not without first making him sweat a little for putting them both through hell this last year! There would still be the question of his profession, but Shannon knew that she could now reasonably accept what had to be until Clinton Wranebow's dream was finished. She would still worry, but with Mitch beside her once more, she could face anything. A life without that curly-headed, blue-eyed, dimpled doll was her only fear at the moment!

She could see that a light was still on in room 26 as she pulled into the motel. Parking her car next to Mitch's, she snatched up the weiners and marshmallows and ran to the door.

Mitch answered on the first knock, his face expressing anguish, then relief when he saw her standing there in the dim lights of the motel. He had been so afraid that she wouldn't come to him tonight. For the last thirty minutes he had paced the floor arguing with himself whether he should go to her and ask her to remarry him or let her come to him. The latter was only fair, he had reasoned, since she was the one who had childishly blown up and asked him for a divorce! No, he would not crawl on his hands and knees to get her back. At least not yet. He had been willing to give her another thirty minutes before he went back to Jerry and Marla's and made a fool of himself. So when he had heard her car drive up, he had sagged against the door in relief.

"Shannon," he said, making his voice sound as aloof as possible, "what are you doing here?"

"Hi. Were you getting ready for bed?"

"Yeah, I was thinking about it," he answered smoothly.

"Could I change your mind?" she tempted with her prettiest smile. "I thought since neither of us ate much dinner we could go on an impromptu weiner roast." She held up the package of hot dogs to show her sincerity.

Mitch shrugged his shoulders. "I am a little hungry."

"Good. Can you go now?"

He shot by her and was sitting in his car before she even had completed the sentence.

"I don't think Marla and Jerry would care if we took their boat," Shannon told him as they drove back to the resort under a full moon. "I noticed a lovely gravelbar the other night when we went to dinner that would make a perfect place to build a fire."

"I think I know the one you mean," Mitch said agreeably. "I noticed the same place."

Thirty minutes later the boat was gliding along the smooth waters heading across the lake. When they reached the gravelbar, Mitch moored the boat to a large tree, and Shannon unloaded their picnic supplies as Mitch got a fire started. They had decided to stop on the way and buy a bottle of wine and some cheese to go along with their hot dogs.

Nothing personal had been mentioned between them. Each one was waiting for the other to start the conversation.

"Uhmm . . . those were good," Shannon commented as she licked the remains of her hot dog off her fingers and settled back with her glass of wine. "Want me to cook you a marshmallow?"

"No. You always burn them," he chided as he lay back on the blanket with her.

"I do not. I'm a good marshmallow roaster. When I was a Girl Scout, we used to make these things called 'smors.' "

"What's that?"

"You take some graham crackers, chocolate bars, and melted marshmallows and smash them all together. We used to make ourselves sick on them. One night we even spread peanut butter on top"—she laughed—"and I was sick for two days!"

"You had me drooling until you threw in the peanut butter." Mitch grimaced. "I don't care if I never taste another drop of peanut butter as long as I live."

Shannon set her glass of wine down and scooted over closer to him. The night was beautiful, with a soft breeze blowing in off the water. Showers of sparks lit up the night as the fire sizzled and popped warmly. Gathering her courage, she leaned over and kissed him.

"What's that for?" Mitch asked a little later as she ended the kiss slowly.

"Uhmm . . . I just felt like kissing you. Do you mind?" she asked, still placing soft kisses around his mouth.

"Not at all," he agreed, his arms tightening their embrace. They kissed again, this time more ardently.

"I should be mad at you," she teased, nipping playfully at his ear when they finally came up for air.

"Me? Why?"

"Well, you left earlier this evening without saying good-bye to me personally," she whispered petulantly as her hands worked at the buttons of his shirt.

"I said good-bye to you," Mitch protested, kissing her lightly down the slim column of her neck. He sensed that she was getting ready to make her move, and he was more than ready.

"Is saying 'night, folks' your idea of telling me good-bye?" Shannon scolded as she peeled back his shirt and buried her face in the thickness of his broad chest.

"Hey, I kept waiting for you to give me some sign that you wanted me to say good-bye in a different way," Mitch reminded, his mouth taking hers again in a series of long, languid kisses.

"I wanted you to," she murmured when she could as his hand slipped in her blouse and gently undid the clasp on her bra. "I—there's things I think we need to talk about before we both go our separate ways Monday."

Mitch's hands paused, then with a soft moan, they enveloped the sweet breasts he had bared. He had no intention of making this any easier on her, at least not for the moment. She had put them both through misery the last year, and she needed to stew a little!

"Mitch, are you listening to me?"

"Yeah, I'm listening," he responded as his mouth gently kissed one of her breasts hungrily.

Shannon groaned and closed her eyes as his mouth sent waves of ecstasy surging through her. She wanted to open the door for his apology, but at the moment he was making it next to impossible for her to think coherently.

"Mitch, don't you think we might have been a little hasty?" Shannon whispered, moaning softly again as he intensified his assault on her senses. His hand tugged at the clasp of her jeans as she willingly slipped out of the binding fabric. And in a few minutes they were both naked, pressed tightly to each other as their kisses grew more demanding.

"Hasty about what?" he pursued in a husky voice moments later as he kissed his way down the satin length of her body, pausing at her navel to tease her playfully with his tongue.

"You know . . . about the divorce," she prodded.

"I didn't ask for it." he pointed out curtly as his mouth trailed back to her breasts. "You did."

"I know . . . but I've been thinking lately. Maybe we both should have been a little more patient."

"Yeah, probably." He kissed her again deeply, his tongue joining with hers in sweet reunion.

Shannon's mind was whirling as they lay locked in each other's arms, their kisses growing more heated by the second. She was giving him every opportunity to admit that he had been wrong about the divorce, too, but he seemed to be waiting for her to eat the whole crow!

"Don't you want to say something?" she asked as her hands ran smoothly over his bare buttocks, her fingers bringing moans of pleasure from him now.

"As a matter of fact, I do," he said huskily.

Shannon smiled smugly. "Well?"

His mouth kissed its way up to her ear and paused as he whispered something shockingly indecent to her.

"Mitchell!" she scolded as he chuckled and moved his

mouth back down to capture hers once more. "Be serious!"

"I am serious," he scolded back, pressing the proof of his words suggestively against her bare stomach.

"Mitch, don't you care that our marriage is over and after Monday we may not see each other ever again?" she pleaded softly against his lips, determined to bring him to his knees.

"Of course, I care, but it's over. What can I do about it?" he said philosophically as his tongue traced the outline of her lips seductively. "I'm more than willing to listen to any suggestions you might have on how we can get ourselves out of this mess," he challenged diplomatically as his hand came up to stroke her intimately. He felt reasonably sure it wouldn't be long now before she would admit that the divorce had been all her fault, and then he could magnanimously forgive her and get on with the good stuff.

This was not going at all like she had expected, Shannon thought resentfully, as her body turned to liquid jelly and she surged helplessly against his muscular frame.

Her hands returned his boldness, and with a low moan, he moved to cover her body with his. Apologies would have to wait until later, they both conceded silently as he once more joined her body with his. There was no problem in the world that could override their need for each other as they soared together in harmony, each one joyously giving of themselves to please the other. All too soon, their bodies demanded and sought fulfillment as Mitch brought them to the peak of their desire, and they both slid over in a wild burst of uncontrollable passion.

As they lay exhausted in each other's arms, the sounds

of night filled their world now as they gently exchanged loving kisses.

"That was nice," Mitch whispered contentedly against the sweetness of her mouth.

"Uhmmm . . ." Shannon agreed, still rather disturbed about his lack of repentance.

"Now, what were we discussing before we got so deliciously sidetracked?" he prompted, ready to bring the conversation back around to their problem once more.

"I don't know. My mind seems to have gone blank." Shannon sat up and reached for her jeans.

"Now, come on!" Mitch looked at her sternly. "We were talking about our divorce."

"Oh?" Shannon glared at him coolly. "Was there something you wanted to say about our divorce?"

A familiar stubbornness invaded Mitch's features. "Not necessarily, but I was under the impression *you* had something you wanted to say!"

"Me? Where did you get that idea?" she scoffed disgustedly.

"Then all this was—was just a damn weiner roast?" he asked incredulously.

"Throw in a couple of damn marshmallows, and you've got it!" she said irritably. If he didn't love her enough to tell her he was sorry, then he could go suck a grape!

"Shannon . . ." Mitch stood up and held out his hand pleadingly.

She turned to face him, forcing a lump back down in her throat. "What?"

They stared at each other in the moonlight, each one

silent as they tried to find the words to say what they were feeling.

"Look . . . I want to see you again before we go home," Mitch told her quietly, breaking the silence.

"I don't see any point in it," she returned in a hurt tone. She continued to put her clothes back on.

"When are you planning on leaving?" he asked softly as he dressed.

"Some time Monday."

"Early? Late?"

"Late in the day," she returned quickly. She wanted to allow all the time she could for him to come to his senses.

"All right, we may not get a chance to talk together, alone, the next couple of days, but I'll try to make it a point to check with you before we go home," he said aloofly as he started to kick gravel on the fire to put it out.

"About what?" she asked as she gathered up the remains of their picnic. What was left to talk about? He wasn't about to admit he was wrong, and due to his stubborn attitude, she wasn't either!

"About . . . hell, I don't know what about! I just said *maybe* I'll check with you before I go home. And, maybe I won't!" he snapped.

"Well, maybe I'll be there, and, then again, maybe I won't!" Shannon snapped back as she brushed angrily by him on her way to the boat.

"You said you weren't going to leave until late," he reminded her sharply as they both climbed back in the boat and he started the engine.

"If you have anything you want to say to me, you'd better say it now," she warned ominously.

170

"When I have something to say to you, I'll be the one to decide when I'll say it!" he stated arrogantly.

And with those two terse statements, they sped back across the lake, neither one budging an inch.

CHAPTER TEN

Although the weather was still hot, the atmosphere between Mitch and Shannon had a definite chill to it during the long Labor Day weekend. They tried to keep up a pretense of amiability in front of the family, but their facade was a false one and was easily seen through.

Shannon was so miserable that she had to will herself to carry on normally during the daytime hours, but at night she was able to let her reserve down and cry herself to sleep. All hopes of a reconciliation seemed to be dashed as Mitch continued to virtually ignore her, spending the majority of his time with either Jerry or his mother.

There were times when Shannon wanted to hold back the hours, dreading the moment when she would get in her car and go back to St. Louis, but when Sunday night finally arrived, she was almost relieved to be packing her bags for the trip home the following day.

Mitch had barely said two words to her Sunday evening, and the "will you please pass the catsup" hardly gave her room to hope that he wanted to make amends.

As she crawled between the cool sheets for what she knew would be another sleepless night, the image of his familiar face surfaced in her mind. She lay staring up at the ceiling, her thoughts torturing her with the way his hair curled so tightly around her fingers. Even when she closed her eyes, she saw the clear, steel blue of his adoring gaze after they had just made love, and the way his dimples would flash so mischievously when he would tease her. She could almost feel the strength of his arms wrapped around her as they slept, the warmth of his breath on her cheek. . . .

Angrily tossing off the light sheet, Shannon rose and began to pace the floor. All of their past arguments, shouting matches, and strong disagreements flooded her mind now, but they were quickly deluged with memories of the wonderful, joyous times they had spent together. And there had been so many of them. Many, many more good times than bad. Honesty prevailed during the long, restless night, and by the early hours of Monday morning, Shannon had learned a valuable lesson. Life at its best is uncertain, but if a person could spend that life with someone they love, then it was worth all the risks that had to be taken. At least for her it was. The divorce had been a stupid, foolish mistake on her part. She had done a lot of growing up in the last year, and she was now ready to be the wife that Mitch deserved. If it meant dying a little each day when he went to work, then that's the way it would have to be. At the moment it was much easier to live one day at a time than to borrow a bushel of trouble from tomorrow.

The hands of the small clock on Shannon's bedside table showed her that it was barely six in the morning as she stripped off her nightgown and threw on some jeans and a T-shirt. In another five minutes she had brushed her teeth and hastily run a comb through her hair.

There was virtually no traffic on the road this early in the morning as she sped eagerly toward Mitch's motel room. He would still be sound asleep, she mused, but she would wake him up and make him listen to reason. They were made for each other, whether he liked it or not, and she was determined that before the day was over, he was going to like it!

Shannon was so deep in thought that when her Porsche topped the last hill before she turned off to the motel, it was fairly flying. Her eyes widened as she saw a fast-approaching car meeting her head on. Swerving the wheel wildly, she headed for the nearest ditch at the same time the other car shot past her. A loud squeal of brakes shattered the quiet of the tranquil hillside as both cars ground to an abrupt halt.

Shannon was still trembling when her car door was thrown open and an angry Mitch stuck his head in. "What in the hell do you think you're doing! You were driving like a wild woman!" he shouted.

"Don't shout at me!" she fumed back, gradually regaining control of her frayed nerves.

"What are you doing out here at this time of the morning?" Mitch demanded, dragging her out of the car to face him. The sun was just barely beginning to shed its light on the new morning as they glared at each other angrily. "You were going back to St. Louis, weren't you? After you told me you wouldn't be leaving until late this evening! Well, I think that's pretty dirty, Shannon!"

"I was not! I was coming over to visit *you!*" she shot back hostilely. "And, what are *you* doing out this early?" Her eyes surveyed Mitch's appearance. His shirt was stuck haphazardly into a pair of wrinkled trousers; he had on shoes with no socks; and she noted with dismay he hadn't bothered to shave yet this morning. "You look like some wino just in off the streets!"

174

"Don't start with me this morning, Shannon. I've had a hell of a night, and I'm in no mood for a sparring match."

Shannon's face grew troubled. "Are you sick?"

"Yes! I'm sick and tired of this game we've been playing!" His eyes blazed savagely in the early rays of sunlight.

"I am too," she shouted back. "That's what I was coming to tell you!"

"I don't care what you say," he raged, completely ignoring her words, "you can't stand there and tell me that you're not still in love with me because I know that's a lie! This last week should have proven to you beyond a doubt that the divorce was a mistake, and if you weren't so darn stubborn, you'd admit that and we could get on with our life!"

"I know it! That's what I was coming to tell you," she stated in exasperation.

Ignoring her words, Mitch pointed his finger at her sternly. "Don't take that tone of voice with me! Everything I've said is true, but it's clear you're going to make me get down on my hands and knees and crawl to you. Well, all right! I'm crawling, Shannon! I love you, dammit, and if that's what it takes to get you back, then I'll crawl from here to—"

Shannon reached up and clamped her hand over his mouth. "I said, I know it! You don't have to crawl anywhere, Mitch. That's what I've been trying to tell you," she said patiently.

Mitch's blue eyes grew suspicious as they peeked out over her hand.

"I was coming over to tell you exactly the same thing, darling. The divorce was all my fault and I'm sorry. I

175

love you, and I don't care what your job is!" she exclaimed sincerely. "It's me that should do the crawling."

Mitch groaned and swept her into his arms. "Oh, damn, don't tell me I'm dreaming. Please, don't let this just be a crazy, wonderful dream," he pleaded huskily as he buried his face in her hair.

"It isn't a dream, darling. I love you, I love you." Her words were smothered by his mouth capturing hers ravenously. They kissed heatedly, each one trying to draw the other one closer to their awakening bodies.

"Let's go back to my room," Mitch murmured in a ragged voice.

"That would take too long," Shannon groaned, her mouth exploring the hollows of his neck.

"I still have the blanket in my car from the weiner roast," he whispered suggestively.

She smiled agreeably. "I'm all yours."

Arm in arm, they got in his car, and Mitch drove down a winding, secluded road overlooking the lake. The blanket was spread on the ground and their clothes discarded in moments, and once more they were locked in each other's arms.

"Remind me to tell you how very much I love you, later," Mitch said as his hands explored her body lovingly. "Because right now all I can think about is showing you."

"We do have a lot of things to talk about," she reminded him as his mouth met hers again and again, "but, I admit I can't think very straight right now, myself."

They made love impatiently, eager to please each other in every way. The shafts of early sunlight fell across their bodies as Mitch carried them to a plane of awareness that they had never experienced before. Moments before they reached the pinnacle of their passion, Mitch moaned and pulled her tightly against him, murmuring words of love in her ear as they crested together, sending waves of shuddering fulfillment coursing through them.

It took a while for them to float back down to earth. All the while, they exchanged lingering kisses and murmured intimately to each other.

"You know, I didn't mean to drag you off to bed the minute I saw you again," Mitch apologized between kisses. "I wanted to do everything properly this time, but . . ."

"You don't need to apologize. I probably would have suggested it if you hadn't. Although I know how you hate pushy women," she teased lightly.

Mitch chuckled softly. "Not all pushy women." His tone grew serious. "Let's face it. I'm a one-woman man. I've never been happy going from bed to bed like some men do." He rose up on his elbow and grinned at her boyishly. "Sorry."

"I'm crushed," she said in mock offense.

"Really? I thought you might be getting hungry."

"Hungry?"

"Well, I hate to say this, but it seems like all we've done since we've been down here is eat and work our buns off!"

"And throw in a little hanky-panky and you've just about described our summer."

Mitch laughed. "Not necessarily in that order."

"Well, I don't know. It's been eat, make love, eat . . ."

"Let's change the format to make love, eat, make love . . ."

177

Another round of kisses followed their playful bantering.

"Well, I'm waiting," he finally said patiently.

"For what?"

"For you to propose to me. I figure we can get married sometime this week and spend our honeymoon down here. You can be spared a little longer from your job, can't you?"

"I suppose so, but . . ."

". . . but, you're still worrying about my job," Mitch said tiredly.

"No, I'm not worrying about your job. I've come to the painful conclusion that I can't love with you, and I certainly can't love without you."

"You mean 'live'?"

"No, I mean 'love.' " She grinned sheepishly. "If you were a kamikaze pilot, I would still have to remarry you."

"That's nice to hear, but I think I should tell you that when I go back I'll be going back to a plain, old, boring desk job. I figure the only thrill I'll have in life from now on is coming home to you and a houseful of screaming kids."

Shannon sat up and looked at him. "What do you mean?"

"I mean, the job has been running so well since I've been gone, it's made me realize that they don't need me to get it finished. I talked to my foreman yesterday and told him that from now on he was the head honcho on the job, and I would take care of things from behind my desk." He reached over and ran a finger down the softness of her cheeks. "This isn't anything new, Shannon. I have always intended to keep my promise to you."

178

"But I thought after the divorce that you probably considered that promise invalid."

"Hey"—he tipped her face up to meet his—"you want to know something? I've never once thought of the divorce as final."

Shannon smiled, tears of happiness welling in her eyes. "What did you consider it?"

"Only a minor setback." He grinned tenderly. "No one is going to take my girl away from me. You should know that by now."

"I love you, Mitchell Wranebow," she stated solemnly as they kissed once more.

"I know you do, but a fellow could grow impatient waiting for a proposal, you know," he whispered as his hands found her breast and stroked it gently.

"Sorry." Shannon sat up straighter and took his hand in hers. "Mr. Wranebow, would you do me the honor of becoming my husband once again?"

"How's your job situation? Do you think you can afford to support me in the fashion I would love to become accustomed to?"

"I think I can give you a few reasonable luxuries," she promised thoughtfully. "A cold beer occasionally, and a clean bed to sleep in each night."

"And, will you be good to me? Now, you understand, I'm not asking for myself, but I know that's going to be the first thing Mom will ask when she finds out we're going to remarry," he said in mock seriousness.

"I'll be good to you," she promised, reaching over and gently pushing him back on the blanket. "I hate to dash your hopes, but your mom has already given me carte blanche with you."

"My own mother sold me down the river!"

Seconds later she was lying on top of him, delighted at how quickly he could be aroused. "Does this mean you accept my proposal?" she asked as her hands caused his breathing to become ragged in record time.

"I accept," he murmured as he brought her mouth down to meet his slowly. "You know something; you're sure beginning to remind me of a pushy redhead I know!"

The loud joyous pealing of the bells nestling in the tall steeple of the Old Wilderness Church could be heard for miles around as they echoed over the quiet Ozark hills on this warm September afternoon. Shannon stood outside the entrance of the rustic chapel, nervously clutching her bridal bouquet of apricot miniature roses and baby's breath, watching the last few remaining guests trickle into the church.

The sweet, melodious sounds of the organ filtered out quietly as Marla reached up to adjust the wreath of roses and baby's breath Shannon wore in her hair. This was the third time Marla had adjusted the hairpiece since they had arrived at the church.

"Will you stop your fidgeting!" Marla scolded lovingly. "You're making me a nervous wreck!"

Shannon glanced toward the direction of the parking lot, anxiously awaiting Mitch's arrival. "He isn't here yet, Marla. What if he decides the remarriage is a mistake?"

"That's when I'll eat my hat." Marla laughed, adjusting the slender gold cross Shannon wore at her neck. "I've stumbled over him for the last week every time I turned around, and you're worrying that he's not going to show up!" she scoffed.

"I don't know," Shannon said skeptically, her brown

eyes trained toward the parking lot. "Maybe he's decided
. . ."

"Just dry up!" Marla shook her sister's shoulders
gently. "He's probably trying to help Jerry into the car.
He'll be here. I'd bet my life on it."

Shannon's eyes grew concerned. "Are you feeling
okay?"

Marla smiled. "My legs are a big shaky, but I feel
fine."

Shannon's stomach fluttered nervously as her eyes returned to the parking lot. Where was he?

As if Marla could read her silent thoughts, she let out a
relieved sigh. "At ease, baby sister. Take a look at what's
coming down the walk!"

Shannon glanced up quickly, her face breaking into a
radiant smile. Walking down the vine-covered path were
two very tall, very handsome men in chocolate-brown
tuxedos with matching apricot shirts. One was limping,
his hand gripping a cane steadily, while the other one
strode briskly down the path, his twinkling blue eyes
searching in quiet adoration for his bride.

"Just look at that," Marla said in awe. "Can you believe those two gorgeous men really belong to us?"

Shannon's brown eyes glowed with love as she met the
blue-eyed gaze of the approaching groom. "I'm beginning
to," she whispered happily.

Mitch and Jerry stopped in front of the two women as
Marla jumped protectively in front of the bride. "Don't
come any nearer!" she warned. "It's bad luck for the
groom to see the bride before the wedding."

"Is that the truth?" Mitch grinned arrogantly, stepping
around Marla and gently pushing Shannon up against a

spreading oak tree. "Jerry, take care of your wife, will you, while I take care of mine?"

Shannon smiled happily as their eyes met lovingly.

"Hi, beautiful," he whispered as his mouth came down to capture hers in a welcoming kiss.

It was several minutes before Shannon pulled apart from his masterful embrace. "Hi. I was beginning to get worried about you," she confessed between soft brushes of his lips.

"Me? Why?"

"I thought you might have changed your mind."

Mitch raised his head, his eyes turning serious. "Not on your life, sweetheart. I've waited for this day a long time."

"You two are going to have to break this up," Marla warned as she pulled away from her husband's arms. "You guys are going to have us looking like a mess!"

Jerry leaned on his cane and grinned at his wife flirtatiously. "You complaining?"

"Certainly not." She wrinkled her nose at him. "Now go away!"

Mitch stole one last kiss from his bride-to-be as he leaned over and whispered in her ear, "I'll see you at the altar, Mrs. Wranebow."

Casting one last, longing look at her, Mitch winked, then turned and walked happily into the church. A few minutes later the organ rang out with the loud strains of the *Wedding March*.

Taking a deep breath, Shannon lifted the hem of her pale apricot gown and followed Marla into the church. Moments before she started down the aisle, she closed her eyes and prayed fervently, "God, please bless this marriage and let it endure a lifetime . . . this time."

With a radiant smile she stepped firmly out into the aisle, eager to seal her vows with the man she was so hopelessly in love with.

The ceremony flew by with Shannon holding on tightly to Mitch as they exchanged vows in steady, unwavering voices. After the endless handshaking in the receiving line, they cut the wedding cake and drank champagne toasts to each other. Happy well-wishers kept them separated from each other during the next hour. Shannon kept looking around the room longingly for her husband, their eyes searching each other out. As Katherine was reminding Shannon of a particular chicken and rice casserole that Mitch loved, he caught her eye, motioning for her to meet him outside.

Excusing herself for a moment, Shannon hurried out the side door, colliding with Mitch, who had her in his arms instantly.

"I thought you'd never get here," he grumbled as he kissed her ardently. "Let's get out of here."

"I don't know if it would be proper to leave our guests this soon," Shannon murmured, matching his heated kisses.

"I'll make it proper," he said firmly. "Follow me."

It took very little time for them to say their hasty good-byes and run for the car amid a shower of rice and confetti. Shannon threw her hands up in despair and laughed when she saw the traditional graffiti written on the car.

"That's horrible," she teased Mitch as they got in. "It looks like something you would have dictated!"

"If *I* had dictated it, you wouldn't have ridden in the car!" he teased back with a suggestive wink.

"Where are we going?" Shannon asked as they pulled

out of the parking lot. She wrapped her arms around Mitch's neck seductively. "I hope it isn't too far."

"Not far at all," he assured as he drew her closer. "You didn't marry a fool!"

They hadn't driven very long when Mitch turned off the main road and drove down to Cedar Lane boat dock. Switching off the key, Mitch reached over and kissed her again. "Come on, baby, I'm about to make all your wildest fantasies come true!" he drawled wickedly.

"Oh, are we going to stay here at the lodge for our honeymoon?" Shannon asked, following him out of the car.

"Nope. We're going to stay in that." He pointed to a sleek cabin cruiser moored at the dock. "A friend of Jerry's loaned it to us for the week."

"Really?" Shannon asked excitedly. "Oh, Mitch, that will be wonderful!"

Reaching for their bags in the trunk of the car, Mitch retrieved the luggage, and together they walked down to the boat.

The expensive, luxury cruiser slipped quietly through the still waters, heading for a secluded cove. Shannon stepped out on the deck as Mitch cut the motor. A brief shower had fallen while they were crossing the lake, making the deck slippery and wet.

Stepping gingerly across the bow of the boat, Shannon let out an excited squeal as a magnificent rainbow arched its brilliant colors directly across the cove, seemingly meant as a wedding gift for the happy couple! To her, it seemed like a perfect omen to begin their new marriage.

"Mitch! Come here quickly!" she shouted.

Shannon heard Mitch drop the anchor with a thud and

the sound of his footsteps flying across the deck. "What's the matter?" he shouted.

"Nothing's the matter, Mitch. Mitch, watch out . . ." she warned as he came skidding by her on the wet deck, shooting straight off the boat into the lake.

"Mitch!" she yelled exasperatedly, leaning over the bow of the boat and watching him finally come to the surface, gasping for breath. "I *told* you to watch it! The deck's slippery from that little shower we just had!"

"What in the hell were you yelling at me about? I thought you had fallen overboard," he bellowed.

"Heavens, no! I just wanted you to see this beautiful rainbow," she said brightly. "Isn't it just beautiful!"

"Yeah, simply breathtaking," Mitch grumbled as he tried to knock the water out of his ears. "You realize that I probably just ruined a three-hundred-dollar tux, don't you?"

"Well, it wasn't my fault," Shannon said in a superior tone. "If you can't keep from falling out of a boat, don't blame me."

"Oh, really?"

"Yeahhhh, really!"

"Come here and help me back in the boat," he called good-naturedly.

Shannon leaned over the boat and offered him her hand. "Next time, you'll learn to listen when I—Mitchell Wranebow!" she gasped as he pulled her headfirst into the lake to join him. She was mad enough to spit nails when she finally surfaced moments later.

"You . . . you . . ." she sputtered.

His laughter filled the quiet cove as he swam over to her and took her in his arms, covering her sputtering mouth with repentant kisses.

"How can a man have a honeymoon if his wife's not with him?" he reasoned as she continued to berate him soundly. "I was getting lonesome without you, Bright Eyes."

"Just look what you've done to me," she cried, pushing her wet, straggling hair out of her eyes. "My lovely wedding dress is ruined."

"You won't ever need it again," he promised with a happy smile, drawing her back into his arms.

"You promise?" she whispered tenderly, draping her wilted headpiece of roses and baby's breath on his soaked, curly head.

"Cross my heart and hope to die." He grinned, displaying those enchanting dimples of his. "But I've been thinking. There's one more set of vows I should have insisted on besides love, honor, and obey."

"And what, pray tell, would that be? I thought the ceremony was perfect."

"Well, I figure if we are going to live together the rest of our lives, I need some assurance of protection for my life, property, and general well-being."

"Okay, spit it out, Wranebow, what do you want from me?"

He leaned over and kissed her mischievously. "I was thinking something along the line of, 'Will you, Shannon, love, honor, and obey this magnificent, generous, long-suffering man *and* swear by all that's holy that you will never can another green bean or cook another pot of okra as long as ye both shall live?' "

Shannon sighed as she laid her head on his shoulder and looked up happily at the rainbow. "I do humbly promise!" she gurgled as he dunked them both under the water and kissed her soundly, sealing their unorthodox vows.

Yes, there was no doubt in their minds that love was alive and very well at Wranebow's Inn!

CANDLELIGHT
Ecstasy Supreme

$2.50 each

Candlelight Ecstasy Romances™

$1.95 each

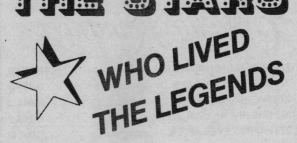